THE VERY THOUGHT OF YOU

CHARLES TOWN BRIDES

BOOK NINE

ID JOHNSON

For Brenda

CONTENTS

CHAPTER ONE

"ARE WE READY YET?"

Kate Woods and her fiancé, Paul Bryant, chuckled as her daughter, Holly, kept urging her to hurry.

"We're getting our coats on," she told her. "We can't very well go out in the snow without them."

Paul draped hers over her shoulders lovingly as his son, Cooper, expressed the same impatience. "It's only next door," he said. "We can just run over real quick."

"And we'll fall on the icy sidewalk doing so," Paul insisted. "So, we're going to wear our coats and walk over carefully."

Cooper pouted slightly, but Kate knew that wouldn't last long on Christmas Day. She could understand the rush since they'd just eaten a light breakfast, and neither child had opened any gifts yet.

They were saving that for the celebration next door at Paul's brother's home. Casey Bryant and his wife, Isabelle, lived in the amazing buttercream colored Queen Anne home next door which looked like it came straight out of a Christmas card, especially when every detail of its gorgeous architecture was outlined in festive Christmas lights.

It was a lot larger than Paul's home, which would be their home in just a week when they got married on New Year's Eve. The idea of living there made tingles of excitement rush through Kate's veins. Kate didn't care about the size of her home, just the people who lived in it.

"Now we're ready," Paul declared, zipping up his winter coat.

"Yay!" both children called out.

Kate and Paul laughed as he took her hand and led the group outside and toward his brother's home. Having just snowed on Christmas Eve, it was overcast out, so the Christmas lights shimmered against the fresh blanket of snow which crunched below her feet.

Casey opened the door as they approached. "Merry Christmas!" he shouted as they hurried to get out of the cold, crisp winter breeze.

"Merry Christmas!" The greeting was repeated by everyone as they went inside where Kate noticed the scent of cinnamon and fresh bread.

"You look lovely," she said as she greeted Isabelle, who was wearing a festive green dress. "Do you need some help in the kitchen?"

Isabelle shook her head. "No, thank you," she said. "Shirley just whipped up some turnovers for a quick bite before we open gifts."

"Wonderful," Kate said. "They smell incredible." She looked back at her daughter who had already plopped down next to Cooper by the giant Christmas tree that was surrounded with colorful gifts. They petted the white, fluffy cat, Princess, and started guessing what the gifts could be. Kate smiled as she watched Paul sit nearby to convince them not to touch anything yet.

It was going to be so nice having a father figure for Holly again, not to mention being married to a wonderful, godly man like Paul. They had both lived through tragedies when their former spouses passed away, her husband Vaughn from an accident and his wife Tonya from an unexpected illness. Losing a parent had been hard on both Holly and Cooper, but now, God was giving them a second chance at having a loving family.

"He's so good with her." Isabelle's soft whispering brought Kate out of her thoughts.

She turned and smiled. "He's the best."

Shirley came in from the kitchen with a plate containing a warm turnover cut into sample bites, and they all tasted one. "These will be for dessert later, and I made enough for the seniors today," she said.

"They're delicious," Kate said, and everyone agreed.

They opened the presents, with the children going first. Both children excitedly tore into theirs and were surprised by some of the more expensive items. The adults exchanged their gifts after that, and Kate was impressed with the beautiful new sweater Isabelle and Casey bought her.

"Thank you so much," she said.

"You're welcome," Isabelle replied. "I saw it and thought of you instantly."

"It's perfect."

Once done with everyone's gifts, Isabelle and Kate brought some hot cocoa in from the kitchen, and they all sat around admiring their gifts and chatting.

"Oh, it looks like we forgot one," Casey said.

Isabelle looked at him with a furrowed brow. "No, I don't think so." She looked around as though she were taking inventory of the gifts they'd given.

"Mom, I think I left it at your house," he said.

"Oh, yes. I think you did." Shirley had a smile on her face that said she knew exactly what he was talking about.

Casey put on his coat and went outside, presumably to Shirley's lovely little cottage Casey had built for her in the backyard. He returned with a box with a handle and holes on the top.

Isabelle gasped. "Casey, what did you do?"

He chuckled and set the box in front of her, which she quickly opened, pulling out a fluffy calico kitten. "Oh, my goodness!" she exclaimed.

"Wow!" Holly said, running over to pet it.

"Is it a boy or girl?" Cooper asked, not far behind her.

"It's a girl," Casey said. He looked at Isabelle. "I thought Princess might like a new friend."

Isabelle cuddled the kitten close, and her eyes twinkled with tears. "She's beautiful," she said, handing the kitten to Holly and putting her arms around her husband. "Thank you."

They exchanged a quick kiss while Cooper picked up Princess and brought her over. She let out a little hiss, sniffing the kitten for a few seconds before walking away.

"Well, she'll need some time to adjust," Casey said. "I'm sure they'll be friends as she gets used to her."

"I know she'll love her," Isabelle said. "I do!"

She and the children played with the kitten, and they all looked so happy as they tried to decide on a name. Finally, they agreed on Duchess to go with Princess. Kate made a mental note to talk to Paul about getting a pet for the family once they were all together. Both Holly and Cooper were old enough to be responsible for caring for either a dog or a cat.

A while later, Casey arranged a spare room with supplies for the kitten to keep it separate from the older cat while they did their Christmas Day service at the senior assisted living home, helping to serve the Christmas meal and entertain the seniors. They all bundled up and headed over, with Kate, Paul, and the kids in one car and Isabelle, Casey, and Shirley in the other.

Other than some light Christmas music playing, the senior assisted living home was quiet for a day that should have been filled with families celebrating with their parents and grandparents. Kate hoped that was because many of them had gone to their families' homes for the day, but she knew there would be several left behind without any relatives to celebrate with them. It made her sad to think that anyone would be alone at Christmas, especially since she was so fortunate to have Paul and the children, as well as so many friends in Charles Town.

A young blonde-haired woman wearing scrubs walked up to them as they entered. Her smile was engaging, though her eyes looked a bit puffy and tired. "Merry Christmas!" she said cheerfully. "I'm Sandra. Which of our lovely guests are you here to see?"

"All of them," Paul said with a chuckle. "We're here to help with lunch."

Sandra's eyes brightened. "Oh, that's wonderful! You must be the Bryants."

"Yes, we are," Kate confirmed. She wasn't technically a Bryant for another week, but they already felt like a close family.

"Perfect! Follow me." Sandra led them all through a maze of hallways that all looked the same, but eventually, they ended up in a cafeteria that smelled of roasted turkey and freshly baked bread. She caught the eye of someone in the kitchen area and waved her over. "This is Audrey," she said as the older woman approached. "She's in charge of everything in the kitchen, so she'll direct you." She turned to Audrey. "These are the Bryants. They're here to help serve dinner."

Audrey smiled. "Well, it's more like lunch as far as the time goes, but it's really Christmas dinner," she said. "I'm so glad you're here. Not many people take the time on Christmas Day to come help out, and we're a bit understaffed."

"We'll do whatever you need us to," Casey said. His eyes scanned the room, and Kate followed them when she saw them brighten at the sight of an upright piano over in the corner. Kate smiled, knowing what her future brother-in-law would ask next since he loved to play.

"Would the guests like dinner music?" Casey asked. "I can play that after we get everyone served if you'd like."

"If you can play it, you're more than welcome," Audrey said. "It'll add a little festive ambiance, I think."

"He excels at ambiance, especially when it's Christmas music," Isabelle said with a proud smile on her face.

Audrey got everyone set up to serve the different dishes. The cooks had made a full traditional Christmas dinner, complete with turkey and stuffing, mashed potatoes, green bean casserole, cranberry sauce, and fresh-baked rolls. Everyone got stationed at a dish, with Holly at the front to help people with their plates and trays.

The seniors started arriving, and they all smiled at Holly, who was exceptionally helpful with the seniors in wheelchairs who had difficulty with their trays. That freed the nurses up to bring in more seniors, so the dining room filled up quickly.

Once everyone had their dinner, Casey went to the piano and started to warm up.

"You're all welcome to have a meal for helping," Audrey said.

"Thank you," Kate said. "The children are probably hungry." She laughed as their fast nods agreed with her statement, and she had them fill their plates and eat at a small table in the corner.

"You too," Paul insisted, picking up a plate and handing it to her. He dished out what she indicated she wanted then fixed a plate for himself. They sat with Holly and Cooper.

As they ate, Casey started playing Christmas carols on the piano.

"We need a singer," Paul said.

"I'll do it!" Holly said.

Kate nodded. "I think that would be nice," she said. "You've been doing very well in your choir practice."

Holly got up and started singing as she came up behind Casey, who looked a little surprised but didn't miss a note as he kept playing "The First Noel," now with an accompaniment. Kate smiled at the scene. As Holly's future stepfather's brother, Casey would be part of the family Kate was about to build for them when she said, "I do," in only a few days. She couldn't think of anything that would make her happier.

The song finished, and Casey moved on to play "O Holy Night," one of Holly's favorites. Kate felt the moisture well up in her eyes as her daughter's beautiful voice echoed across the cafeteria. After that song finished, they moved into the upbeat tempo of "Jingle Bells," and Holly walked through the seated seniors, encouraging them all to sing along. Pretty soon, everyone was laughing and singing Christmas carols well after they'd finished their meals.

Kate and Isabelle served everyone cake and ice cream for dessert, and the singing stopped for a while, but one of the nurses got up and told the story of Christmas. After that, they all visited with each table for a while, hearing stories of Christmases past from people who had lived long enough to see so many of them.

As they drove home, Kate felt exhausted but filled with joy in her heart because she knew they'd made the day more special for everyone in the assisted living facility.

"How come I feel so happy?" Holly asked. "I didn't even get to play with my presents much yet."

"Because Christmas isn't about presents," Paul explained. "They're just a symbol to remind us of what God gifted us—life and love. You feel happy because you've given your time to others, and that's what it's all about."

Kate smiled at him, feeling the excitement build for their wedding in just a few days. While she had to get in her car and go home tonight, this would be the last Christmas that would happen. After New Year's Eve, they'd go home together as a family from now on.

After taking a few gifts but leaving the rest behind since they'd be moving in his house soon anyway, Holly ran in for one more thing, leaving Kate and Paul standing in the driveway next to her car.

"Text when you get home," he said, his voice leaving steam in the crisp air.

"I will." She looked at the house and smiled. "This time next week, this will be our home, too."

"I can't wait," he said and leaned in for a gentle kiss.

CHAPTER TWO

Sophie

"Everything is so beautiful." Sophie Kemper held onto the railing of the luxury yacht, looking out at the bright blue ocean and lush island greenery.

"I'm glad we booked this day cruise," her new husband, Dr. Zach Kemper, said as he wrapped his arm around her.

"Me, too," she agreed. "I think we picked the perfect spot for our honeymoon. We should come back here every year."

"I'm game if you are." He gave a chuckle and kissed her cheek. "Although, if we start having a family in the next few years, it might get more challenging."

She nodded thoughtfully. "Right, though it would be a lovely spot for a family vacation as well. But that'll be in a couple of years after I finish my early childhood education degree."

"Of course," he agreed. "You might even want to give that another year while you start your new job, but we can play that by ear."

She nodded and turned as the cruise director got everyone's attention. The energetic young woman made everything sound like an adventure, and Sophie figured it really was. Being out in the ocean touring the islands felt so far away from their everyday life in Charles Town. It was wonderful seeing a part of God's creation that was so different from what they experienced in West Virginia.

"For those of you participating in the snorkeling dive, we'll be at our location in about thirty minutes," the woman said. "Please follow me if you're ready!"

Just about everyone on deck followed her, and they were all introduced to a dive instructor who went through the basics and safety protocol. Sophie was a little nervous, but a squeeze of her new husband's hand calmed her. She couldn't wait to see all the amazing sea life that wasn't visible from the surface.

The ship anchored offshore while everyone got their equipment on, and soon, Sophie and Zach were stepping off the back of the ship and into the water where they swam over a bit with the rest of the group before beginning the snorkeling.

The view took her breath away with so many different colors and shapes among the coral reefs. It was an interesting experience, communicating underwater with her new husband, who kept pointing to fascinating coral shapes and colorful creatures. A few times, she saw things he didn't notice, and his eyes went wide when she would show him something unique.

After a while, they returned to the ship for a light lunch as the ship moved on for more of the tour. The seating was arranged so everyone could eat while watching the view and listening to the cruise director talk about the history and geography of the island. All of it was interesting, and Sophie relaxed as she sat with Zach in the warm, gentle breeze.

By the time they got back to the port, they had about an hour before dinnertime.

"Let's do some shopping," Zach suggested. "We have time to get a few things and take them back to our room before our reservations."

"I'm all for that," Sophie said with a laugh. "I promised Lexi I'd get her something from Fiji."

"Then we'd better get working on it," he said.

The resort had a long line of cute shops with souvenirs, art, T-shirts, and other items. They held hands as they explored each one.

"Oh, look at this," Sophie said, picking up a small figurine of a dolphin posed on some type of clear blue stone. "Lexi would love this." Her co-worker, and best friend, Lexi had also bought her a figurine on her own honeymoon.

"I think she would," Zach agreed. "Let's get her that. If you find something else when we shop more, we can get her more than one thing."

Sophie nodded and they took the figurine to the cash register, but not before she tried on a couple of sun hats for their beach plans the next day. They returned their purchases to their room in the luxury resort and got ready for dinner.

"I sure am glad things are so casual here," she said. "I got a little sunburned on that cruise, so I think the straps of my formal dress might hurt."

He shrugged. "We can always buy you something different here. In fact, I'm sure we will."

They both laughed as they headed to the restaurant where they ordered seafood plates.

"How long do you think you'll stay on at the dental office?" he asked her. "We'll need a few months to hire a replacement." As the primary dentist there, Zach planned on continuing his work while Sophie moved on to her career in early childhood education. While she loved her job and the people there, she wanted to do something different than dental assisting.

She nodded, finishing up her bite. "I guess until I finish the degree, or if I find something else. Isabelle is keeping an eye out for openings at the preschool. I'd love to do that part-time while I'm in school."

"That would be perfect," he agreed. "This shrimp is delicious. It's so fresh."

"It's good, but I'm looking forward to dessert." They both chuckled, knowing her love of junk food. She always had chips or pretzels or some other snack around, and she really adored sweets.

She wasn't disappointed with the chocolate torte for dessert, which she savored while they kept chatting.

"I'm so glad we got our winter wonderland Christmas wedding," she said. "I loved having it outside in the snow rather than in the building. I can't wait to see the video and the pictures. Jake said they'd be ready in less than a week, so he'll send them to my phone to take a look." She was glad they hired Jake, the photographer, who had done such a great job with some of the other recent weddings they'd had in their group of friends. There was only one wedding left—for Kate and Paul—and unfortunately, she would miss that one since it was happening on New Year's Eve in just a couple of days. Lexi had promised to video as much as she could and take pictures while everything happened so she wouldn't miss it completely.

After dinner, they went back to their room. Their luxury suite was spacious and beautiful, with a small, private infinity pool right off their deck that seemed to go right into the ocean. With built-in seating, it was the perfect place to watch the sunset.

"This is so unbelievably gorgeous," she said as they sat together in the warm water.

"So are you." He smiled at her and gave her a light kiss.

She giggled when they pulled apart. "Why thank you, husband."

"It's all true, my beautiful wife," he said.

She felt tingles of joy at the title, something she'd waited so long for. After their breakup when he went through a dark time when he found out his former friend was responsible for his first wife's death, she'd wondered if they'd ever be sitting together like this as husband and wife.

She looked up at the sunset, thinking about how their future was a wide-open space just like the colorful sky before her. She enjoyed her job as a dental assistant, but she knew when she trained for it that it wasn't exactly what she wanted. As a single woman, her goal at the time was to find a field that paid well and allowed her to work with people. As she started to work with the children in the dental office more, she realized how much she loved being around kids. Her friend Isabelle, a kindergarten teacher, helped her choose her early childhood education program, which she would start in January.

The sun finally disappeared behind the ocean in a breathtaking last minute of beautiful streaks of color throughout the sky. Now, it still glowed from its light, though the colors of the sunset were gone.

"I'm not used to it being so warm at night," she said.

He chuckled. "Me, neither. It's a lot different than our snowy wedding."

She laughed with him, leaning against his shoulder in the warm water. "It's a lot different, but both things are wonderful."

THE NEXT DAY, THEY DID SOME MORE SHOPPING AND ATE A QUICK lunch before heading out to the beach in front of their resort, which provided covered cabanas with restaurant service. There were several couples around, but the cabanas were spread out for privacy. They sat in the comfortable lounge chairs the resort provided and laid back next to each other, looking at the bright blue expanse in front of the white, sandy beach.

"Well, this is definitely relaxing," Sophie said after a while.

Zach sat up and turned toward her. "It is, but that water is calling me."

She chuckled, sitting up. "It does look nice and warm, doesn't it? I guess there's no point in coming to a beach if we're not going to get our feet in the ocean."

"Let's go," he said. "I'll race you!"

It took her a moment to realize what he'd said, but when she did, she jumped up, throwing off her cover-up robe and running toward him. He was obviously letting her catch up, but she passed him by anyway and laughed all the way to the water. The waves were gentle, and she threw off her flip-flops right at the water's edge, letting the warm, moist sand sink through her toes.

He caught up with her, and she felt herself being lifted up, giving her a shock for a moment until she felt his warm chest against her as he carried her further into the water. Zach set her down, and they laughed and splashed each other, which made Sophie laugh even more. After a little swimming, they went back up to their chairs under the umbrella, drying off just as a staff member from the resort brought out some colorful blue mocktails with pineapple chunks in them.

"Mm, this is good," Sophie said. "I'm glad you ordered these."

"They're a little sweet for a dentist, but I figured why not? It's our honeymoon," he said.

She nodded, taking another sip from the slim straw. "It's our honeymoon, and we should both enjoy it as much as we can."

They spent all afternoon at the beach, even ordering dinner in the cabana, this time steaks instead of the seafood they'd been eating for the past few days.

"So, I haven't thought to ask you yet, but what did you think of my wedding dress?" she asked after finishing a bite.

"It was incredible, and you looked like a princess walking down the aisle in the snow," he said. "That cape was a good idea for the cold. The fur really made it work for a winter wonderland scene. It looked like part of the dress."

"That was Penny's idea, the woman who owns the bridal shop," she said. "Valerie thought to ask her what to do about the cold the night before, and they brought them to us that morning–a little late." She giggled. "I was so panicked that morning before Valerie got there."

"I bet," he said. "But it's all a beautiful memory now."

"It's the most wonderful memory of my life," she admitted.

"We'll make more beautiful memories together every day now." He reached out his hand to grasp hers.

"That's for sure," she agreed. "Now we have a new future ahead, including my new career working with children."

"You're going to be so wonderful at that." He smiled.

"I really do think it suits me better," she said. "I am going to miss everyone at the dental office, though. I've met a lot of friends there. It's always a lot of fun chatting with so many different people."

"Well, maybe you can still visit on your lunch breaks," he

suggested. "None of the preschools are very far away from the office. I'm sure Lexi would still love to chat with you and giggle about your junk food habit."

She laughed. "That's true. I'm sure I can stop by now and then. Of course, Lexi might not work there forever, either."

He shrugged and turned toward the ocean. The waves were picking up a little, creating a gentle, soothing sound in the background. "I'm sure it'll be a while before she goes anywhere," he said. "Lexi likes her job, and there's no reason for her to leave."

CHAPTER THREE

"I can't believe I found out I'm pregnant on Christmas Day!" Lexi Renfro was still so excited that she could barely contain herself. Everything had changed in that instant she stood with Max, her husband, staring at the test strip, watching the second line form.

But even though she was sure the home pregnancy test was right, she still wanted to hear it from the doctor to make it official. She could barely sleep at night waiting to find out if the doctor's office was open the Monday after Christmas. Her dental office was closed for the whole week, so she wasn't sure what would be happening at her doctor's office. Finally, the day came, and she called as soon as she could. She felt like jumping up and down when the receptionist answered instead of the answering service.

"Good morning," the cheerful woman said. "How can I help you?"

"I'd like to make an appointment as soon as possible," Lexi said. "This is Lexi Renfro."

"Oh, hello, Lexi," the woman said. In a small town like Charles

Town, everyone got to know each other pretty well. "You're in luck. We have an opening on Thursday."

Lexi frowned and was glad the woman couldn't see her. She wasn't sure how she was going to stand waiting until then. "Thursday," she repeated, and Max frowned as well. "Okay, I'll take it," she said.

"What are we seeing you about?" the woman asked.

"I think I'm pregnant!" Lexi couldn't help but say those words excitedly.

"Oh, that's wonderful!" the receptionist said. "Um… Lexi, can you hold for a moment?"

"Sure." She wasn't sure why she needed to hold if she was going in on Thursday, but she waited, listening to the soft cello music on hold.

The woman came back after a moment. "Lexi, can you come in today?"

"What? Yes!"

"Madge was on the other line with a cancellation," the woman explained. "We'll see you at two today. Does that work?"

"Yes! I'll see you then!" She said goodbye and hung up, looking up at her confused husband. She couldn't help letting out a giggle. "Someone was calling in a cancellation at the same time. We're going at two!"

His eyes brightened. "Wonderful! What on earth will we do until then?"

Lexi laughed. "I have no idea. I'll probably sit here and be a nervous wreck."

He let out a chuckle. "We can't have that. I'm pretty sure those home tests are really accurate now, so we probably have nothing to worry about. Why don't we go see a movie? They have some classic movies still playing over at the little theater."

Lexi wasn't sure she could pay attention to anything, let alone a movie, but it would give them something to do besides sitting there staring at the walls and getting herself even more nervous. "Sounds good," she said. "A little buttered popcorn sounds pretty good right now."

Max let out a chuckle as he pulled out his phone to check the movie times. "Okay, there's another one starting in an hour. I guess they're still showing Christmas movies. *It's a Wonderful Life*—do you want to see that one?"

She nodded. She liked that movie, though she didn't expect she'd be able to pay much attention to it. "That sounds good."

Lexi went to change her clothes and put on some light makeup. A few minutes later, she went downstairs where Max helped her with her coat. Soft praise music played on the radio as they drove to the theater, and Max bought tickets as they walked inside.

It was fun, sitting in the theater munching on popcorn with extra butter, watching a good movie, but Lexi couldn't get her mind off the tiny life she was sure was growing inside her. There was so much responsibility to being a mother. She knew she was willing to put all she had into it, but she wasn't sure whether that would be enough.

Max brought her out of her thoughts with a whisper. "I see you over here overthinking things. Just enjoy the show, and enjoy this new chapter in our lives."

She smiled and nodded, trying to get all the worry out of her mind so she could focus on the positives, that God had given them the greatest gift they could imagine, which meant He trusted they could do the job well. That thought made her feel better as she enjoyed the rest of the movie.

It was nice, taking time during the day together on a weekday. She was always so busy commuting to Charles Town from their home in Shepherdstown, and he worked full-time at the historical society. This week, he was on vacation, and she was only working sporadically at the emergency dental clinic in town.

When the movie ended, it was time to start heading to the doctor's office. Lexi's excitement grew the closer they got—now they would know for sure. As Max had said, she knew the home tests were pretty accurate, but felt like it would be more real when she heard it from a doctor.

He held her hand as they walked into the office, where she was greeted warmly. "It's been a while!" the receptionist said. "So, I need you to fill out this paperwork."

Lexi nodded as she took the clipboard and sat beside Max, trying to stay relaxed while she filled it out.

"Lexi Renfro?"

"That's me," Lexi said when the woman called her name. Max held her hand again as they walked through the door, at least until she needed to step on the scale and get her temperature taken. With that all done, the nurse led them to the exam room.

"So, it looks like you suspect that you're expecting," she said as she closed the door.

"Yes," Lexi confirmed. "I took a home test, and it was positive."

"Wonderful! Well, we'll go ahead and confirm it here," she said. "Let me get your blood pressure, then I'll send you down the hall to get a sample."

Lexi nodded, sitting in the chair and wondering how many digits over normal her blood pressure would be from all the excitement. When it was pretty close to normal, she was surprised. The nurse ushered her back to the restroom for her sample while Max waited in the exam room. She tried to hurry, and soon she was back in the exam room with Max standing beside her holding her hand.

There was a knock on the door, and her doctor walked in. Because it was a small town, everyone called her Dr. Mary, though that was her first name. She preferred the less formal title.. Lexi looked at her expectantly.

"Well, congratulations to you both!" she said, and Lexi felt her heart thump in her chest. "Though you were expecting that, correct?" Dr. Mary continued.

"Yes," Lexi said. "But hearing it from you is so...."

The doctor nodded with a smile. "I know what you mean."

Max gave Lexi a tight hug.

"Do you need a minute?" Dr. Mary asked.

"Um... no, that's okay." Lexi stepped back from Max, though they kept their arms around each other. "We were expecting it, though it is exciting."

"It's wonderful news," the doctor said. "We just need to go ahead and get some blood samples so we can see how things are, if you're up for it."

Lexi nodded. "Of course." What she really wanted to do was get up and dance around celebrating, sort of the way she felt at their wedding, but she held still while the nurse came in and took some blood, a few more vials than she was used to giving, which made her a little lightheaded. That passed quickly, and the doctor moved on to talk more about the pregnancy.

Dr. Mary pulled out a calendar. "Okay, we estimate you at seven weeks pregnant," she said. Lexi felt more tingles of excitement. "We calculate full gestation at forty weeks, though some births occur as early as thirty-seven and are still considered full-term. So, minus your seven weeks, forty weeks from today is… August sixteen."

Lexi reached over and grasped Max's hand. "Wow, that's a long time."

The doctor chuckled. "Yes, it is. But it'll pass relatively quickly, and this time next year, you will have just celebrated your baby's first Christmas!"

"Oh, my goodness," Lexi exclaimed. She hadn't thought about that because she was so nervous about whether she was pregnant or not in the first place, but it was such an amazing thought. The next Christmas morning, she and Max would wake up together and hold their child in their arms while they enjoyed Christmas morning together.

"That is so fantastic," Max said, one of the first sentences he'd gotten out since Dr. Mary confirmed the pregnancy. Lexi knew he was just as excited as she was.

"It is a miracle," the doctor agreed. "I do wish I'd specialized in obstetrics on days like these. It would have been a joy to deliver your baby. But I need to refer you to the OBGYN we partner with, Dr. Jennifer Williams. She's amazing. I know you'll both love her."

"I'm sure we will," Lexi agreed.

"Hang out here for a moment, and I'll have someone come in and get that appointment set up, and she'll give you a sheet with our recommendations for prenatal vitamins, diet, and other things," Dr. Mary said. "Your exam went great, and you seem very healthy. If I see anything on the blood work you need to be concerned about, I'll let you know. And we'll forward those results to Dr. Williams."

"Thank you so much," Max said. "You've given us the best news ever."

The doctor smiled. "You're going to be wonderful parents. Take care, and the nurse will be in shortly."

"Thank you," Lexi said before the doctor walked out. "August sixteenth!"

He nodded, a big, toothy grin on his face. "August sixteenth," he repeated.

"I can't wait to find out if it's a boy or girl," she said. "I forgot to ask how soon we can see that."

He shrugged. "I'm sure the nurse will know. We'll ask her when she comes in."

"Oh, yeah," she said. "I'm just so excited, I can barely think." She laughed.

"I'm feeling the same way," he said. "We're definitely going out to dinner to celebrate. But when will we tell everyone?"

She thought for a moment. "I don't want to overpower Kate and Paul's wedding. It's in two days. Why don't we wait until after that?"

He nodded. "That makes sense," he agreed. "Are you going to text Sophie?"

"I want to so badly, but I think I'd rather tell her in person," she said. "I think I'll wait until she comes back. Maybe we can take them both out to dinner and tell them together."

"That sounds like a wonderful idea," he said.

The nurse came in and gave her the information sheet and answered a few questions, including when they could find out the baby's sex. "It really depends," she explained. "That's usually in the second trimester, though the baby's position when they do the ultrasound makes a difference."

"When is the second trimester?" Max asked.

"Thirteen weeks," the nurse explained.

That felt so far away for Lexi, but she knew she had to be patient. They got all the information and made the OBGYN appointment then went out to their car.

"I think a prayer of thanks is in order," he said as he got into the driver's seat.

"Definitely," she agreed. They'd prayed about the baby more than a few times since the home test came out positive, but she felt especially thankful today.

They bowed their heads. "Lord, thank you for the blessing of this child," he began. "Life is the greatest miracle You give to us, and we are so thankful that You bestowed it on us. We will do our best to be the best parents we can so the child can grow up to live a godly life in Your service. In Jesus' name we pray, Amen."

"Amen." Lexi opened her eyes and looked at her husband, feeling tears welling up. "Goodness, there's so much to plan for," she said. "Should I keep working?"

"For now, you can if you want to," he said. "My income is solid, and I put a lot of money down on the house so the payments are low, so you can decide when you're ready."

It was all so wonderful and overwhelming at the same time. But most of all, Lexi was so unbelievably happy.

She was going to be a mother.

CHAPTER FOUR

Olivia Nix sat at her desk in her home office, staring at her computer. Up on her screen were several boxes of character descriptions for the story idea she'd worked hard on putting together for her newest novel, but none of them fit her mood.

That was because she was pregnant and had only found out about a week earlier, before Christmas and Sophie and Zach's wedding. Knowing there was a child growing inside her was incredibly distracting, and all she wanted to write about was babies.

The problem was that none of her new characters were anywhere near being married, so babies wouldn't fit into her storyline yet. She'd designed her newest title before she knew about the baby, and she'd worked so hard on it that she didn't want to start from scratch. But with Christmas over just days ago, New Year's Eve on the way, and the baby to think about, she wasn't in the mood to work, though she'd really wanted to have a head start on her planned work for January.

So, she decided to start small, maybe just working on the first chapter so the rest could start falling into place. She made it about halfway through before looking down at her belly and resting her arm protectively over it. Her general practitioner, Dr. Silverberg, had assured her that everything was fine because her first appointment with her new obstetrician, Dr. Biesen, wasn't until after the New Year's holiday. Still, she was a little worried she wasn't doing something right, so she pulled up her browser and searched "early prenatal care" for probably the hundredth time.

She was lost in reading the results of that search when her husband, Memphis, walked in.

"Do you need anything?" he asked.

She had to giggle, and she clicked out of the browser. "No, thank you," she said, "not since you asked five minutes ago."

"Just checkin', Olivia," he said in that wonderful Texas drawl of his. She loved hearing him speak, especially when he said her name.

He was off work for the holiday week and had planned to get started on the nursery. It was a bit early for that at only a few weeks in, but they'd both been so excited that they'd gone to the paint store and picked out a light buttercream shade that would work perfectly whether they ended up decorating for a girl or a boy. The problem was, he seemed just as distracted as she was and kept checking on her every few minutes–like now.

She pushed back her ergonomic office chair and walked over to him, reaching up to put her arms around his neck. "I'm fine," she insisted. "And it's going to be a long nine months if you're worried about me every five minutes." She gave a chuckle to show she was teasing. She loved that he was so attentive.

"I'm just worried and excited." He bent down and placed a gentle kiss on her lips. "It's hard on the husband, too, you know. I'm supposed to protect you and our child, but there's not much I can do in that department at the moment."

"I know." She smiled. "There's not much I can do, either. We both just have to wait while God makes this baby develop, and that takes time." She dropped her arms and sighed. "And I can't focus on writing, either. Maybe I can paint the room with you."

He shook his head. "Oh, no. You're not goin' anywhere near those paint fumes, young lady."

She laughed. "I guess that really is a bad idea. But I want to help decorate."

"Once the paint's dry, we'll do it together," he suggested.

"Deal." She nodded. "I don't like the smell of paint anyway." She turned as the antique grandfather clock in her office chimed on the half hour. "It's a little early, but we could have some lunch. Are you hungry?"

"Always." He let out a chuckle. "You know I'll never turn down food."

She giggled again as they went down the hall to the kitchen, one of her favorite rooms in the house. It was huge, and she'd spent a lot of time and money getting it exactly as she wanted it, in an elegant European design. She'd shopped around for a long time, trying at least a dozen places before she found the right marble countertops and beautiful cabinets. And the space was so large, it was perfect for all the get-togethers they hosted so all her friends could congregate in the kitchen, and she could bake whatever she wanted to in her professional-grade ovens.

But now, it was just the two of them. "What do you feel like eating?" she asked.

"Just something easy and quick, sweetheart," he said.

"I still have some of that roast beef you like. Would you like a sandwich?"

"Perfect."

He got down some plates while she gathered the bread and other supplies, and he leaned on the counter while she made the sandwiches. "Maybe it's just the holidays, but I don't know how I'm going to work while I'm pregnant," she said after a while. "I'm so distracted, and all I can think about is the baby. I need to piece together each scene in my head before I can write it, but my head is just… full of babies." She laughed.

"You don't have to work," he said. "You still have plenty of royalties coming in from your other books. Maybe you need to take a break."

"Maybe." She plated his sandwich and sliced it diagonally. "But I also need to keep myself busy, or I don't know how I'll stand waiting nine months."

She placed her sandwich on a plate, and he carried them both to the dining room table where they both sat. "You don't have to stop working completely," he said. "Maybe set some part-time hours for yourself, and then the rest of the time you can spend with friends or shopping or something. Then, take a couple of weeks off here and there. You're already tired. Maybe as you get further along, that might happen more. Think of it as a pause now and then while you focus on the baby when he or she needs you."

She nodded, finishing a bite of her sandwich. "That makes sense. I'm really glad I didn't go on that book tour. I would have been exhausted."

"Me, too," he agreed. "I would have gone nuts knowing you were pregnant and so far away."

"I don't know how I'll ever do another one of those, honestly," she said. "How can I be away from you and the baby?"

He shrugged. "Maybe we can make family vacations out of them. I'm sure we'll work it out."

"That does sound nice."

She started to stand, but he put out his hand to stop her. "Whatever you need, I'll get it."

"I was just going to get us some milk," she explained.

"Two glasses of milk coming up."

She had to laugh again as he walked away. "Thank you," she said when he came back with their drinks. "But I do still like doing things by myself. I'm only a few weeks pregnant. When I get bigger later on, I'll probably need your help. But for now, you really don't have to wait on me."

"I like bringing you things," he said. "But I get it. I'll stop hovering like a helicopter."

The phrase made her giggle again. She was in such a good mood, knowing her dream of becoming a mother was finally coming true. "I don't mind hovering. Just leave me a few things to do myself."

"You've got it."

They finished eating and lingered quietly together at the table for a while. "I'm wondering if I need to change my story," she said eventually, breaking the silence.

"Why?"

"All I can think about is babies." She let out a chuckle. "My characters aren't even married yet, so that's out of the question. Would people want to read books about married couples starting families?"

He shrugged. "I'm no expert, but I think people like to read about life, whether it's something they've experienced or something they think they want to experience. I know a whole lot of people who want to have babies, so why wouldn't they read books about that?"

"I guess you're right," she agreed. "Maybe after I finish this one, I'll show what some of my characters' lives look like after the happily ever after. There's so much wonderful stuff that can happen after most of my stories end."

"Then that's what you should do. Can I get you anything more? Are you still hungry?"

She laughed. "You're doing it again, Memphis," she said. "But no, thank you. I'm fine. Why don't you start on the baby's room? I can't help you with it until the painting is done, and I really want to start decorating it. In the meantime, I'll go work on my Bible reading for Kate and Paul's wedding. I have some more ideas to add to make it a little different. Theirs is a second-chance wedding. I think I should find more ways to celebrate that."

He kissed her on the cheek. "Okay, but I'll take care of these dishes." They both got up, and he carried the plates to the sink.

"Deal." She paused in the hallway for a moment, watching as he rinsed the plates and loaded them in the dishwasher. He was the perfect husband, and she was so blessed that God had sent him her way.

She went back to her office and got settled in, clicking out of her writing program and pulling up the document for her Bible reading for the wedding. She rested her elbow on the desk and her hand on her chin, trying to think of the Bible verses she knew about second chances. Most of the ones she could think of were about getting a second chance from God after sinning, and they didn't fit. So, she looked the topic up and found some beautiful words in Lamentations 3:21-23.

That was fitting, she decided. Kate and Paul had both fallen into despair when their spouses passed away. It was God's compassion that brought light to their lives and led them to each other. They needed God's compassion and the hope of His love to get them through. With tears welling in her eyes thinking about what her friends had been through, she wrote some introductory words to explain why she'd chosen that passage. After that, she would move to some of the more popular Bible passages to read at weddings.

Once again, she put her hand to her belly, wondering if there was a little boy or a little girl developing there. What a beautiful wedding she would help plan one day if it was a girl. She'd saved her wedding dress and hoped one day her daughter would love it as much as she did. If it was a boy, maybe one day his bride would consider wearing the dress.

There was so much ahead for them, now that they were starting a family. She chuckled, realizing that fast-forwarding to their son or daughter's wedding was a bit of a stretch. There was so much that needed to happen first. She and Memphis hoped to have many children. They'd all take their first steps, say their first words. Then there would be school, and friends, and all the sports or dance classes or musical instruments they wanted to play. Then one day, they would graduate, and Memphis and she would take pictures of all their children in their caps and gowns.

But there she was, getting ahead of herself again. She giggled and went back to her document, adding some nice words about how anything is possible with God's love.

She went back through it, correcting all her typos and re-writing a few paragraphs that were a bit awkward for reading out loud. Then she practiced it, reading it to the computer until it felt just right.

Smiling, she felt good about her work and decided to take a break and go plan something for dinner. Her phone dinged, and she looked around on her desk for it before finding it. She chuckled at the text from Memphis.

'Can I get you anything?' it read.

CHAPTER FIVE

Erin Farrell smiled as her husband, Luke, stood behind her and fastened the lovely silver Irish cross necklace he'd bought her for Christmas. When it fell into place, it sparkled against the green dress she was wearing for her doctor's appointment that day, which also matched her bright green eyes and complemented her auburn hair.

There was no denying she was pregnant, being a few weeks late for her period and most definitely experiencing morning sickness. They'd been hoping for a child, confident now that they were ready to start their family. As a counselor who worked with children, she'd been thinking a lot more lately about having children of their own.

So, she'd made an appointment with an obstetrician directly rather than going through her regular doctor. She was ready to do more than just verify her pregnancy. She wanted to get to know the person who would be with them through those nine months of waiting so she could be comfortable with them when it came time to be in the delivery room. She was also hoping, in the back of her mind, that the obstetrician could do something that allowed her to see or hear their baby.

She'd also chosen the same obstetrician, Dr. Bailey, who cared for her sister-in-law, Valerie, who had found out she was pregnant a few months ago. Erin was so excited, thinking about the cousins growing up together. It was wonderful to experience it all at the same time as her brother, Alec, and his wife. It was also fun because her friend Olivia was also pregnant, probably a bit closer to how far along she was, so they could also share the experience together.

"You are so beautiful." He wrapped his arms around her while talking to her in the mirror's reflection. "If we have a little lass, I know she'll look just like you."

She smiled, loving his Irish accent that always brought the same giddy reaction from her. "Do you want a girl?" she asked.

"I want whatever the good Lord blesses us with," he said. "I just wish Ma were around to see the little one as well."

She turned around and wrapped her arms around him. It had been so difficult when his mother had passed away. From everything he'd told her about her, Erin also wished she could be around as they started a family. She'd died before Erin had really gotten to know her.

"We'd better get going," he said.

She nodded, grabbing her purse and heading out to the car and buckling up. They were quiet on the drive over, settling into the calm comfort of each other's company. She wasn't nervous, just excited, being so positive she was pregnant that she'd already looked up everything on the doctor's website about diet and exercise in early pregnancy so she could give their baby the best possible start.

"I guess after this we can tell everyone, except that I don't want to overshadow Kate and Paul's big day," she said as they pulled into the clinic parking lot.

"We can wait," he agreed. "Wouldn't hurt to let your brother and Valerie know first, though."

She nodded. "I've been thinking about that. It'll be fun to swap pregnancy stories with her, so I definitely want them to know first."

"Well, I might give my dad a bit of a hint about it, too," he added.

She laughed. "Of course. We'll tell our families first." His father lived just up the street from them and often came over for dinner. He'd come to America from Ireland after Luke's mother passed, and she was always glad he was so close. She was close with her parents as well, so they'd also get to find out before the rest of their friends.

They headed inside to the clinic where both women at the long front desk were on the phone. The one with jet-black hair smiled and raised a hand when they walked up, indicating she was almost finished.

"How can I help you?" she asked after she hung up.

"I'm Erin Farrell. I have a ten o'clock appointment with Dr. Bailey."

"Perfect," the woman said. "Looks like you're new, so I have some forms for you to fill out."

"Of course." Erin took the clipboard full of papers the woman handed her and sat by Luke, who had already taken a spot near the TV. She moved the pen chain out of the way and started writing. But soon she had to giggle at how interested Luke seemed to be in the cooking demonstration shown on the screen. "Will you make that for me for dessert tonight?" she teased, though she wouldn't have minded if he'd said yes. The apple pastry looked really good.

"If I could, I would," he said, and she knew he meant it.

She finished filling out the forms and turned them in then returned to her seat to wait. After a couple more cooking demonstrations, a bunch of commercials, and an interview with a woman who seemed to have invented some pretty nail polish colors, Erin finally heard her name, and they were ushered back to the hallway behind the door.

"I'm Krista, Dr. Bailey's nurse. I just need you to step on the scale, then we'll get a temperature and head back."

Erin handed Luke her coat and purse and slipped off her boots, not because she was worried about her weight but because she wanted to have the most accurate early pregnancy weight she could get. She'd read enough comments in the pregnancy blogs to know that a lot of women weren't quite sure how much baby weight they were carrying because their first weigh-ins were in the winter, and they were wearing heavy boots.

"All right, follow me." Krista gave them a smile and walked them back to the exam room where she closed the door behind them then sat at the computer and started looking over the screen. "Well, I hope we have good news for you today. Have you taken a home pregnancy test yet?"

Erin shook her head. "No, but I'm fairly certain I'm pregnant. I'm late, I'm feeling morning sickness, and we've been trying for a child."

"All right, let's start with a urine sample then and go from there." Krista shut off the computer and gestured toward the door. "Mr. Farrell, we'll be back in just a few minutes."

Luke nodded as Erin flashed him a smile and followed Krista down the hallway to the restroom. She had to admit, she was starting to feel a little nervous. What if she had these women go through all the trouble of an appointment and then it turned out she wasn't pregnant? The thought hadn't even entered her mind, she'd been so sure.

The nurse left her to do her business, and Erin locked the bathroom door. As she got the sample and placed it into the cut-out cabinet in the wall, she hoped she wasn't wasting everybody's time.

She returned to her room to find Luke standing by the window, peering through the blinds. He startled when she walked in. "Any news?"

She chuckled. "I just gave the sample and came back," she explained. "We have to wait for them to test that, then I'm sure Krista will be back–or Dr. Bailey."

"Right. I knew that."

"What were you looking at?" she asked.

He waved her over and parted the mini-blinds again. The clinic backed up to a residential street, so there was a large house behind it with a field between, all blanketed in fresh-fallen snow. The house was still all decked out with Christmas lights, which were turned on despite the time of day, casting a colorful glow against the snow.

"It's beautiful," she said.

He nodded. "I'm thinking of getting some of those icicle lights for our house next year."

"I'd love that." Erin turned at the sound of a quick knock and the door opening.

A woman she assumed was Dr. Bailey stepped in, wearing a white coat with a beige pants suit underneath. "Oh, you're looking at the Hansens' house. It's lovely, isn't it? I'm Dr. Bailey." She extended her hand, and Erin and Luke both shook it.

"It's beautiful," Erin agreed. "I think my husband is stealing ideas for our house next year."

The doctor let out a chuckle and sat in her revolving stool, scooting over to the computer. She turned to them before pulling up a report. "Well, congratulations are in order!" she announced. "You're definitely pregnant."

An intense set of emotions overcame Erin, first shock and excitement, even though she'd been sure she was pregnant, and then happiness and a twinge of nervousness about what lay ahead. She leaned on Luke, who turned to her and wrapped his arms around her, holding her tight, which helped calm the worry part of it all so she could focus on her happiness.

It took a few minutes before Erin remembered the doctor was in the room. "Oh, I'm sorry," she said.

Dr. Bailey chuckled. "You're fine. Believe me, I know this is a big moment for everyone. I've had people practically walk out of the room, forgetting I'm here." She laughed again. "Would you like to know your due date?"

Erin's eyes went wide. "You know that already?"

The doctor nodded. "I do, based on the date of your last period you gave us, and the fact that you've said you're fairly regular. Right now, we're looking at around August tenth. That might change slightly when we do the ultrasound."

"August tenth," Erin repeated. She looked at Luke, whose eyes were wider than she'd ever seen them, and who didn't seem to be able to speak at the moment. She giggled a little and looked back at the doctor. "Is there any way… I mean, is it too early to hear him or her, or even maybe see the baby?"

"We can definitely listen for the heartbeat," Dr. Bailey said, standing. "I tend to like to do a vaginal ultrasound when we first confirm the pregnancy, just to see how things are. If you're ready for that, I'll step out so you can get into a gown."

Erin nodded, and the doctor stepped out while she slipped into a paper gown while Luke stared out the window at the pretty Christmas lights and put the paper sheet over her legs. Once the doctor came back with the nurse, she lay back so the doctor could perform the ultrasound, holding Luke's hand for support. Though she and Luke had prayed for a healthy baby, she was still a little nervous about the doctor's first look at things.

But when a distinctive, rhythmic whooshing sound came from the machine, all that worry melted away into pure happiness, and she instantly felt tears well up in her eyes.

"There's your baby," the doctor said, smiling. "And everything looks great! Let me finish up here, then we can talk about what's next."

Erin felt the tears slip out of her eyes and roll down her cheeks, and Luke looked at her with a similar glossiness to his eyes, but he wiped her tears away, giving her a kiss on the cheek where they'd fallen.

He finally spoke for the first time since the doctor had confirmed the pregnancy. "Oh, no. I didn't get out my phone and record it."

Dr. Bailey chuckled. "No need," she said. "I hit record! I'll have Krista get you a copy."

After getting answers to all their questions from the doctor, the nurse set up a new appointment, sent them an email of the heartbeat recording, and directed them to go to the lobby after Erin got dressed

A few moments later, Erin stepped into the waiting room in a daze, and the last thing she expected to hear was her name.

"Erin?"

She looked over to see her brother staring at her in confusion, and

Valerie, who'd been sitting beside him, stood as realization seemed to hit her. She hurried over.

"Are you—"

She didn't need to finish the sentence. Erin nodded enthusiastically, and Valerie let out something that sounded like a squeal, wrapping her arms around her in a tight hug. "Congratulations!" she said. "Oh, this is so wonderful. You have Dr. Bailey?"

Erin nodded again, feeling like if she said any words out loud right then, they would just sound like blubbering from her daze of happiness.

Alec seemed to finally catch on. "You're having a baby?"

"Yes!" Luke answered, and the two men shook hands as he offered his congratulations.

Alec turned to Erin, holding out his arms and wrapping her into a tight brotherly hug. "Congrats, sis. This is fantastic. We're all going to be parents around the same time."

"Isn't it perfect, though?" was all Erin could say. She was so happy.

CHAPTER SIX

KATE

KATE PULLED INTO THE BRIDAL SHOP PARKING LOT AND SAW THAT Isabelle and Erin's cars were already there. They'd already done their final fittings, but they both had come along to support her as she tried on her dress one last time before her wedding.

"I can't wait to see you in the dress again, Mom," her daughter said.

"Me, neither." Kate parked the car, and she and Holly headed into the shop. "I'm so glad I went with one of Lois's custom-made dresses. She's so talented." She had to admit she was a little nervous, wondering whether trying on the dress would bother her this time. The mermaid-style skirt was just like the one she'd worn to her wedding with Vaughn, though the rest of the dress was completely different, and the light blue color was obviously not the same.

She didn't mind the first time she tried it on, but now, it was just two days before the wedding, and she thought the proximity might start bringing up a whole slew of memories. She'd warned Isabelle and Erin that might be the case, so her friends were ready to distract

Holly if emotions started to take over, and she needed a moment alone.

But for now, she was all smiles when she saw her friends sitting on the sofa in the lounge area of the bridal shop, chatting with Lois and Penny, the bridal shop owner who collaborated with the seamstress on custom-made wedding dresses.

"Good morning," Lois greeted them cheerfully. "You're going to love it! I think all the issues have been resolved, and we should have a perfect fit."

"Good morning, and I know we will," Kate replied. She greeted her friends and sat with them for a while to chat, noticing that Erin seemed a little distracted. She looked at Holly, who was far enough away admiring some dresses on display that she felt comfortable asking if there was a problem. "Is everything okay?"

Erin nodded. "Yes, I'm fine."

"You just seem distracted," Kate said, accepting a cup of tea from Penny. "Thank you."

Erin bit her bottom lip, pausing for a bit before speaking again. "Okay, I didn't want to bring this up yet before your wedding because I don't want anything to distract from your day. But I guess it's something you need to know."

Alarm washed over Kate, wondering whether there was something wrong with Erin or her husband. "Are you all right?"

Erin nodded her head vigorously. "Yes! I'm more than all right. I'm pregnant!"

It took a beat for Kate to register what she'd just said. "Oh, my goodness!" She stood, meeting Erin halfway as she did the same and enveloping her in a hug. "Oh, that's so wonderful! Congratulations!"

"My goodness," Lois said. "What a blessing."

Isabelle was next with a tight hug. "Congratulations! That's so incredible. Does Alec know? Oh, goodness… does Valerie know?"

Erin nodded again. "Yes, they were actually at an appointment at the obstetrician when I walked out of mine. And we had his father over for dinner last night and told him. And I told my parents as well."

"What's going on?"

Kate turned to see a confused Holly behind her. "We just heard wonderful news," she said. "Mrs. Farrell is going to have a baby!"

"Wow! That's awesome!"

Kate chuckled at her daughter's enthusiasm, but she felt just as excited for her friend. Most of the women in their group of friends hadn't experienced motherhood yet, and since they were all married now except for her, and she already had a child, she was looking forward to making even deeper connections very soon as they all became parents.

"What wonderful news!" Penny, who had gone in the back to get more drinks, walked out with a mug of hot cocoa for Holly. "Well, now there's even more to celebrate."

Erin turned to her and Lois. "I thought I'd try on my dress today, too, to make sure there's no problem with the fit. Not that I'll be showing in two more days, but, you know, maybe I'd be a little bloated or something."

"Yes, you can certainly try it on, but I think your style is pretty forgiving," Lois said. "I'm glad you mentioned it now. We can keep that in mind."

"Thank you." Erin looked at Kate. "See? I'm already being a distraction from your special day. You need to try on your dress!"

"You're not distracting at all," Kate insisted. "In fact, I think it's wonderful that we have even more to celebrate."

"Can I try on my dress too?" Holly asked. "I think it's so pretty."

Kate shrugged. "Why not? Isabelle, let's all have a little fun."

"I'm game," Isabelle agreed.

"All right, I'll go get the rest of the dresses," Penny said. "Kate, your wedding dress is already hanging in the fitting room. I'll be right back."

Once she returned and put the dresses in the fitting room, they all went in, with Kate making sure that Holly didn't spill her hot cocoa. She had her set it down right away on the table to the side of the huge fitting room, which also had a privacy screen and huge floor-to-ceiling mirrors. Her dress was in a garment bag hanging on a rack.

"Okay, please send someone out when you're all ready," Penny said as she stepped out.

"Well, let's start with the bride," Erin suggested. "I can't wait to see it again. Your dress is just gorgeous."

"Lois is amazing," Kate agreed. She stepped up to her dress and unzipped it, hitching a breath when the soft, stunning blue fabric and lace were revealed. So far, she wasn't having any flashes of memory, so she pulled the dress out of the bag and took it behind the privacy screen to try it on.

When she stepped out, everyone smiled. "Oh, my. That's just so beautiful," Isabelle said.

"Mom, you look like a princess," Holly added.

Kate chuckled. "I feel like a princess." She straightened out the fabric around her waist and then looked up into the mirror, a wide smile growing on her face. Yes, the skirt was exactly like the one she'd worn at her first wedding but paired with a completely different bodice and sleeves, not to mention the stunning baby blue fabric that looked wonderful against her strawberry blonde hair.

A few memories popped into her head, but she was surprised to find them pleasant—her mother when she first tried on her wedding dress next to her, her father's little speech before he walked her down the aisle. With the healing love of God and the happiness of knowing she and Paul were about to have a wonderful life together, it was becoming easier to think of her time with Vaughn, and she could look back on those days without crying.

She felt so blessed that God had given her the time she did have with him, and of course, the miracle of their child Holly, and felt even more blessed that she'd been given a second chance at a family with Paul and Cooper.

She brought herself out of her thoughts. "You ladies put yours on, too," she said. "This is a celebration!"

All of them laughed, and one by one, Isabelle, Erin, and Holly tried on their dresses. Then Kate sent Holly out to tell Penny and Lois that they were ready.

"You doing okay?" Erin asked when Holly left.

Kate nodded. "I'm fine. I have memories, but honestly, they are pleasant. I had a great life with Vaughn, and I know Holly and I will have a great life ahead with Paul and Cooper. What's to cry about?"

"You're one hundred percent right," Erin agreed.

They turned to the door as Holly came back in with Penny and Lois in tow. "Oh, how stunning," Penny said. "I've seen it before, and I still can't believe how gorgeous it is, or how wonderful you look in it. Lois, you've done an amazing job."

"Well, thank you," the seamstress said. "Our young lady here is the one who makes it look so beautiful."

Kate chuckled at being called young, though she supposed she was to the two older women. She was the oldest of their group of friends, after all. "Thank you."

Lois checked her dress over, pulling and tugging at it a few times before walking around her one more time. She looked up and smiled. "It's perfect!" she announced. "You're all ready to get married, Kate."

"It feels perfect, and thank you so much," Kate said. "Your work is just amazing."

"Lois, you're talented, that's for sure," Isabelle agreed.

"All right, let's take a quick look at you other ladies," Lois said. She went to Erin first, walking around her in much the same way she had Kate. "I don't think you have anything to worry about. It seems to fit fine with a little wiggle room. You've chosen a great style."

Erin nodded. "Yes, I love it, thank you. It doesn't feel too tight."

"Perfect." Lois looked over Isabelle's dress and then Holly's the same way.

"Well, what a beautiful wedding party you have here," Lois declared. "I think everyone is ready to go for the big day!"

"I love this color, too," Erin said.

"So do I," Isabelle agreed.

"It'll be perfect with the flowers," Kate added. "Macey is mixing my color, your color, and some deeper, rich blues in all the flowers and ribbons, along with white and silver. I'm so excited." She spent a few more minutes admiring her dress. "Well, we'd better get these off so they're fresh for the wedding. Can I buy you all lunch? We need to celebrate that new baby!"

"I'd love to," Erin said. "And thank you."

"I'm in!" Isabelle added.

"Let's get burgers and fries!" Holly suggested.

Kate chuckled. "That sounds good, but let's ask the others. What do you think—Bishop's Diner?"

They all agreed, and they took turns getting out of their dresses behind the privacy screen. Kate paused for a moment before slipping out of hers, wishing she could wear it for a lot longer than just one day. But then she slipped it off and got dressed, hung it up, and they all said goodbye to Penny and Lois, who declined a lunch invitation because they had other plans, and left for the diner.

Bishop's Diner was still decorated for Christmas, and the fresh scent of Douglas fir from the wreathes enveloped Kate as she walked in. It was such a warm, friendly atmosphere, and she was feeling so happy. She'd marry the man of her dreams very soon, and she'd have a built-in son along with him that she already loved very much.

When he was younger, Kate had helped Cooper as he adjusted to his mother's passing. At the time, Paul was quite lost, struggling to deal with his own feelings and barely able to keep up with the responsibilities of fatherhood. Kate knew the feeling all too well. Thankfully, she'd been able to help, along with Isabelle, who was Cooper's teacher at the time, and Casey, Cooper's uncle. With strength from God and the love of good friends, and eventually, each other, the healing process had led them down a wonderful new path toward a new, second chance at a family.

Macey and Sam were sitting at a table and waved them over. There was a bit of an overflow, but the hostess pushed another small table against theirs, and they all sat.

"So, what is the bridal party up to?" Macey asked.

"We had our final fittings," Kate explained. "So, we're out celebrating." She looked at Erin, who nodded. "And we have a whole other reason to celebrate as well."

"Really? What's that?" Macey's question was interrupted by the waitress, and they all gave her their orders. They ate there so often, no one even needed to look at the menu.

Macey turned back to Kate when the waitress left. "So, what do you mean?"

"I'm pregnant!" Erin blurted out.

Macey's jaw dropped, and she got up and walked around the table to give Erin a hug. "That's so wonderful!" she said. "When did you find out?"

"Just yesterday," Erin said. "And yes, Alec and Valerie know, as do our parents."

Kate sat back and relaxed as they all started chatting about the baby and the wedding. She felt so blessed to have such a wonderful group of friends and such a happy life ahead.

In just two days, that new life would begin.

CHAPTER SEVEN

Macey

Last week had been quite a busy one for Macey Abernathy's flower shop, getting everything ready to go for Sophie and Zach's wedding on Christmas Eve along with all the regular orders. But nothing was slowing down yet since she was also putting together flowers for Kate and Paul's wedding on New Year's Eve.

So, instead of being at home relaxing, she was at the shop putting centerpieces together for the wedding the day after tomorrow. But she wasn't alone. Since her husband was off work for the school's Christmas vacation, he'd volunteered to help.

She glanced over at him and raised a brow. "Wow, I'm impressed. You have a great eye for design. Who knew that fifth grade math was an art form?"

"It actually is." He chuckled. "But really, I just get a lot of practice helping with craft days in the church's children's programs."

"You've done a lot of those, haven't you?" She wiggled a wire around to fit a silver ribbon around the flowers in front of her, all in different shades of blue.

"Grace Point has a lot going on for a small country church," he said. "I think I do more there than I did for First Christian. I love it, of course. And I love you."

He gave her a peck on the cheek, which made her giggle. She was proud of her husband for so many things, not least among them being how well he connected with children. Math wasn't always a subject every child enjoyed, but most of them were truly excited about being in his class. He had seemingly unlimited patience both for those who struggled with schoolwork and those who had behavioral issues. He was such a wonderful man. It was hard to believe she'd been blessed enough to have God bring him to her.

"I love you, too," she said. She finished tying the bow and set the centerpiece aside. "Okay, there's another one done. What are we down to?"

Sam turned and bent over to look at the checklist on the table behind him. "Okay, there will be twenty-five tables, and we have—" He turned again to count how many centerpieces were on the large tables in front of them. "Seventeen, so eight more to go."

"Not bad," she said. "I'd like to get these finished tonight and get them in the cool room. These are hardier varieties than what I'm using in the bouquets, which will be last–tomorrow night probably. We can work on the boutonnieres in the morning, along with the arrangements for the altar and the other tables."

"Which other tables?" he asked.

"I'm doing a long display of flowers in front of the cake and then one behind the guest book," she explained.

"That'll be nice." He started adding flowers to the next centerpiece.

"I can't believe this is the last wedding we're having in our circle of friends," she said, starting on another centerpiece herself. "I'm going to miss this. I mean, we have a lot of clients who hire us for weddings, but it's so much fun when it's for friends."

"Well, we'll need to make a few new friends and fix them up so they can get married."

She had to laugh at his matter-of-fact tone. "You sound like Mrs.

Gregory. And actually, now I see why she does it. There's something fun about setting up the perfect match."

He stopped what he was doing with a flower mid-air. "Do you think she set us up?"

"Oh, most definitely, yes," she replied with a chuckle. "I don't know how she did it, but I know she did something."

He laughed and went back to what he was doing. "Well, I'll have to thank her then." He turned to her and gave her a quick wink.

"Me, too."

They worked quietly for a while, just content with being with each other, working on a project with mutual goals. Things had been like that since they'd gotten married, and it felt so right. They had similar tastes and seemed to agree on things most of the time, and when they didn't, Sam's exceptional patience kicked in as he listened to her concerns and tried to find a way to compromise. Maybe it wouldn't always be like that, she thought, but God's choice of a husband for her was certainly perfect.

"It's fun doing this together," she said after a while. "We don't always have this much time to do things like this with each other."

"I think I'll be doing more of this in the summer," he said. "Carl might be handling summer school this year. He teaches science, so he can also handle math. Maybe we can plan a vacation."

"Oh, that would be really great." She worked the ribbon into the centerpiece in front of her. "Where would we go?"

He shrugged. "I don't know. What do you feel like doing?"

"What do you think about a trip to Yellowstone? I'd love to spend some time there." Macey had been there before as a child, but she knew she hadn't really appreciated the beauty of God's creation quite as much as she would now.

"That sounds fun," he agreed. "I do like hiking and being outdoors."

"Let's plan that, then," she said. "I'm getting excited already. Okay, here's the last one." She finished tying the bow. "Help me get these into the cool storage, and we'll get out of here."

"After you," he said, making a grand gesture of waving his arm.

She giggled and picked up two of the centerpieces, carrying them to the back. Sam followed, and they put their works of art on shelves in the cool storage, and Sam wheeled out a cart on the way back to load up the rest. Finally, they got them all into the cool storage, locked up, and headed home.

Fluffy greeted them at the door. "Oh, you were all alone so late," Macey said, scooping the little white Havapoo up into a hug. Fluffy wagged her tail furiously, obviously happy to see them. Sam gave her a hug as well and then set her down, and she scurried to her bed.

"I'm thinking hot cocoa," Macey suggested.

"You're reading my mind."

They both chuckled and went to the kitchen where he took out the mugs while she got the ingredients together and heated the milk. Once both mugs were ready and had an acceptable number of marshmallows, Sam carried them both to their new living room. Their friend, Reid, and his construction crew had added it last year, with more renovations on the older country home planned for the spring.

"I'm so glad Reid had time to fix that door," she said as Fluffy jumped up on her lap on the sofa. She gave her a long pet that included her crooked tail, which was a result of her being hit by a car that Thanksgiving.

"I knew he'd make time for it," he replied. "Everyone loves our Fluffy." The little dog moved over to him and pushed her muzzle under his hand.

"We spend a lot of time at work," she said. "Do you think she gets lonely?"

He shrugged. "Probably. Dogs are very in tune with their owners. I read once that they can tell how long you're gone by how your scent fades."

"Oh, that's terrible," she said. "I wouldn't want to go on vacation without her, in that case."

"We could always ask someone to take her in," he suggested. "Or since it's more of a camping trip, maybe there are some dog-friendly places we can go in Yellowstone."

"Do you think so?"

He shrugged. "Why not? Here, I'll look." He pulled out his phone and looked it up, nodding as he handed her the results. "Look, we can get a cabin where she can stay with us."

"Oh, that would be fantastic." She scrolled through the photos. "It's beautiful, too. I'd love to do that for our vacation."

"When do you want to go?" he asked.

"Probably mid- to late summer," she said. "I get a lot of June brides. Not that Betsy couldn't handle a wedding, but I'd rather not leave her if several come up." Her assistant had been working with her for some time, and there were several girls at the high school who loved coming in to help, but Macey knew that the rush of June weddings could be overwhelming.

"How about the first week of August?" he suggested.

"That works for me. It gives us plenty of time to plan for it."

He took a sip of his cocoa. "Oh, that's really good."

She nodded, taking a drink. "Delaney gave us some of her secret stuff in that gift basket."

He laughed. "Lucky us. She doesn't part with that easily." Their friend Delaney, the owner of the bakery, had a special recipe for Christmas cocoa that she didn't share with anyone, though she did occasionally give some of the powdered cocoa as Christmas gifts.

She shook her head. "No, she doesn't, and this is wonderful."

Fluffy went back over to her and curled into her lap, leaving her crooked tail sticking out. "I'm so glad she's okay," she said. "And poor Leslie was panicked, thinking the worst." It turned out that Leslie Forester, whose car had struck Fluffy when she got out by mistake and ran out unexpectedly into the street, was a neighbor of sorts, or her parents were. After the accident, they'd become good friends, and she'd spent quite a few more Sundays at Grace Point instead of her usual church in town.

Sam was quiet for a moment, sipping on his cocoa. Macey looked over at him and raised a brow. "You look deep in thought," she said. "What's up?"

"Oh, I was just thinking," he began. "Leslie did say she was hoping her boyfriend would propose."

Macey let out a chuckle. "I guess we do have more friends that might be married soon. Hayden does look like a nice man." He'd been accompanying Leslie to Grace Point for the past few Sundays, so she assumed she'd talked him into trying out the small country church Macey loved. First Christian was also a great church with a wonderful congregation, but ever since she first attended Grace Point, she knew that the smaller community atmosphere was more her style. Everyone had such a deep connection there.

"I chatted with him a bit after the service last week," Sam said. "He didn't say it exactly, but I get the feeling he is planning on proposing on New Year's Eve. Well, he was going to have dinner with her parents sometime this week, so I imagine he's talking to her father about asking her."

"That would be wonderful," Macey said. "She's such a sweet lady. It was a bad way to get to know her, with Fluffy getting hurt, but I do think she'll be a good friend."

"Definitely." He took another sip of his cocoa and looked at Fluffy. "Actually, I think I have another idea."

She flashed him a suspicious smile. "Sam-Sam, what other plans for people are going through your mind?" She giggled. "I can't think of anyone else we know who might get married."

He shook his head. "It's not about people." He nodded toward Fluffy. "Do you think she'd like a friend?"

"I think she definitely would," she replied. "What are you thinking?"

"Well, it's almost the new year," he began. "I think there's probably a dog out there who needs a second chance. Why don't we go check out the animal shelter after the holiday and see if we can find a good match for our Fluffy here?"

Her eyes went wide. "Do you mean it?"

He chuckled. "Of course I do," he replied. "I've been thinking about that lately. You're right. We do spend a lot of time away from the house, and she's stuck here alone. I bet she'd love to have a friend."

"And I bet there's a sweet dog out there who would love to have a family," she said. She set down her cocoa and scooted toward him.

He set his own down on the coffee table and wrapped his arm around her and Fluffy.

"That would be so wonderful," she said. "You're such a perfect husband."

"Well, I certainly try."

They both laughed as he held her tightly. She felt so blessed.

CHAPTER EIGHT

Delaney

Delaney Taylor woke up and stretched out her arm to find the space beside her empty. Instead of worrying, she smiled, knowing that Josh had gotten up to take care of the twins. They were getting older now at nine months, so they didn't need quite the level of intensive care they'd required as younger babies, but since there were two of them, it was as if her work was never done.

Not that she minded—their twins, Ethan and Abby, were her everything, a miraculous gift from God she treasured every day. It had taken so long to be blessed with them, with so many difficult IVF procedures and so many months of waiting and disappointment before they finally got the wonderful news. So, caring for them was a dream come true she would never think to complain about.

But it had been several months since sleep was on a normal schedule for her. Even during the pregnancy, there were many nights she was too physically uncomfortable to relax. Getting no sleep was her new normal.

But not today because Josh was taking care of it all. As she rolled over to check the time, she was amazed that it was already eight o'clock. She felt completely rested, a sensation that had become completely unfamiliar to her.

But now, she couldn't wait to see Josh and the children. She pushed the blankets off and stood, wrapping herself in the soft terry robe her mother had bought her for Christmas. The distinctive scent of fried potatoes wafted up the staircase as she headed down to the kitchen.

Josh greeted her with a smile. "Good morning." He averted his eyes for just a second to flip the eggs in front of him but walked over and gave her a kiss on the cheek. "How did you sleep?"

"Perfectly," she said. "Wow. You're really giving me the royal treatment today."

He chuckled and went back to the stove while she walked over to the playpen and picked up their son. "Oh, you're so adorable," she said as he greeted her with babbling coos, reaching his hand out to grab her face.

"They've eaten, and they're cleaned up, changed, and ready to start an awesome new day of being adorable twins," Josh said, still manning the stove.

"Well, that sounds fantastic." She put Ethan down because Abby was reaching up for her, and she gave her daughter a tight hug before putting her back down and engaging them both with toys.

"And your breakfast is ready," Josh announced.

The babies seemed distracted enough by the toys that she stepped back and sat at the kitchen table, where Josh put a full plate of bacon, eggs, and hash browns in front of her. "You're amazing, Josh," she said. "You didn't have to go through all this trouble. Just getting up with the twins was more than enough."

"Well, you need to eat, too, and frankly, this sounded good." He chuckled as he sat with his plate of food, reaching over to take her hand.

She smiled and bowed her head while he said grace.

"Dear Lord, thank You for our family, for the food on our table, and for the many blessings You give us every day. Thank You for watching over our little ones and for blessing us with their lives. We will spend the rest of our lives making sure they grow up to be Your humble servants. In the name of Jesus Christ, we pray. Amen."

"Amen." She looked up at him and smiled. "I feel so well rested. Let's do something fun today."

He nodded. "How about a trip to the aquarium?" he suggested. "That's all inside out of the cold, and they both love to look at fish."

"That sounds wonderful," she agreed. "It's a long drive. Are you up for it?"

He finished a bite of his bacon. "I am. It's my vacation, after all. I think we deserve some family fun."

"That's true," she agreed. "You've been working so hard with the Christmas tree farm. We've had a busy year."

He nodded, finishing another bite. "For sure. I just have some maintenance to do, but that's nothing that can't wait a few days. We thinned out the area around the bigger trees. A lot of the smaller ones sold this year, too. I think your cocoa was the best seller, though."

She laughed. "Well, Nana's recipe does sell out fast at the bakery, too. Oh, a day at the aquarium sounds like a lot of fun. Your parents are watching them for the wedding tomorrow, so we should spend some time with them today."

"Then it's settled," he said. "After I clean up the breakfast dishes, we're off to Baltimore."

She enjoyed her breakfast but hurried a bit. Even going to the store was an adventure with twins, but the almost two hour drive into the city required a great deal of preparation. She got ready quickly, and then, together, Delaney and Josh put together everything they needed, including some of the new toys from Christmas to entertain the children in the car, in about an hour. Soon, they were heading to Baltimore to enjoy the aquarium.

There was no snow in the forecast, and that was calming for Delaney, allowing her to just look out the windows and enjoy the beautiful winter scenery without worrying about getting caught in bad weather. It was lovely, the way the snow blanketed the countryside. Most trees had lost their leaves, but there were a few large fir trees here and there flocked with the bright white Christmas snow.

"I can't wait until next year," she said. "Well, and all the years after that."

Josh chuckled, keeping his eyes on the road. "How come?"

"Because next year, they'll be walking, and after that, they'll be running," she said. "I can't wait to see their faces as they run downstairs on Christmas morning. Won't that be fantastic?"

He nodded, still looking ahead. "It absolutely will be. I can't wait for that, either. We're going to have to make sure we get up earlier than them so we can see it, though."

She let out a chuckle. "So, I definitely can't sleep in like today."

"You deserved the rest," he insisted.

"It was good for me," she said. "Thank you again, so much. You didn't need to add breakfast to the treat, but I'm glad you did. It was delicious."

"You're very welcome," he said.

They were mostly quiet for the rest of the drive, and she enjoyed the scenery more. Eventually, the countryside gave way to higher density development, and they reached the heart of the city, arriving at the aquarium at about lunchtime.

"We'd better eat first," she said.

He nodded. "We'll park first then find a nearby café," he suggested. "I'm sure there's something."

They found a place to eat and settled the twins into two highchairs. They had just ordered when a woman with silvery gray hair walked by.

"Oh, my goodness, twins," she said. "They're adorable."

Delaney smiled. "Thank you. We think so too, but we might not be objective." She chuckled.

The woman laughed. "There's no objectivity about it. They're gorgeous. How old?"

"Nine months," Delaney said. It was hard to believe it had been that long since she was in the operating room for her C-section. Time sure passed quickly, she thought.

"They're so beautiful," the woman said. "What a blessing. Well, you all have a wonderful day."

"You, too," Josh said. "And thank you." He chuckled after the woman left. "They sure attract a lot of attention. We get that at least once every time we go somewhere."

"That's because they're so beautiful," she said.

He nodded. "I agree."

The food came, and it was delicious. The twins were able to eat finger food on their own with just a bit of help. When they were all done eating and cleaned up, they loaded them back into their double stroller and started toward the aquarium. It was busy, as expected during the holiday week, but it wasn't too difficult to get around, so Ethan and Abby could enjoy looking at all the colorful fish.

When Ethan started reaching for one display, Josh scooped him up out of the stroller and held him near the glass. "That's a blue fish," he said. "And that one's yellow."

Delaney picked Abby up and rested her on her hip, telling her about the different colors as well. They switched babies and did the same for the next fish tank then set them back in the stroller to head over to the dolphin exhibit.

Both children seemed to love the dolphins, so Delaney and Josh took them out of the stroller again to sit on their laps and enjoy them. They spent a bit more time there because they could sit and relax, and once again, a few people made comments about how cute they were.

Soon, the twins were tired, so they decided the best thing to do was start the drive home so they could rest in their car seats.

Delaney relaxed, reclining her seat slightly as Josh watched the road carefully. "That was a fun day," she said. "Tiring but fun."

"It was," he agreed. "That's a really good place to take them, especially when it's too cold out to go to the zoo."

"We should go there more often." She took a sip of her bottled water. "I'm so excited about the wedding tomorrow. Kate is wearing a light blue dress. Everyone who has seen it tells me it's gorgeous."

"I'm sure it'll be lovely," he said. "I guess this is the last wedding in our circle of friends."

"Yes." She took another sip. "But now, we get to all hang out as married couples. And eventually, if God sees fit, we'll all have babies that will grow up together."

"That'll be nice," he agreed. "Though Kate and Paul already have a built-in family."

"They'd like to try for more." She looked out the window then back at her husband. "It's just all so wonderful. I'm so happy for them."

"Me, too."

They drove for a while before he spoke again, breaking the silence. "Do you ever miss being in the bakery working?"

She inhaled, having not expected the question. She had two locations now, and she'd left both of them in the hands of competent managers ever since her pregnancy. "I'm happy being with the children, and they need me."

"I know that, but I get the feeling sometimes that you'd like to be in there baking again and being around all the customers," he explained.

"I guess I would, in a way," she admitted. "But I wouldn't trade my time with our children for that. Maybe there'll be a time when they're old enough that I can take them with me to work."

"You could always work part-time once they're in school," he suggested.

"Right, but by then, honestly, I'm hoping we'll have more of them," she said.

He chuckled. "Hopefully, God will bless us in that way. I just know you were really in your element when you were in the bakery. It's how I feel out working on the tree farm. I want to make sure that our lives include all the things that give you joy as well."

She turned and looked at him. His eyes sparkled but remained locked straight ahead on the road. She was so lucky to have a husband like him who always thought about her. He'd shown that many times today—letting her sleep in, cooking breakfast, and now, caring about how she felt about her bakeries. "I love you for that. I'm perfectly content for now."

"I bring this up because I thought of something after you mentioned what the children would be like next Christmas," he explained.

"Oh?"

"Maybe you could bake some special edition cookies in the bakery for Christmas each year," he suggested. "It would get you back into the bakery for a bit. Our parents could watch the children while I'm at work."

She nodded, letting the idea sink in. "I'll think about it for next year," she said. "Actually, that would go great with my Christmas cocoa."

They both chuckled as they continued toward home.

CHAPTER NINE

Kate

Kate pulled into the driveway of Paul's house, and she couldn't help but get excited about how it would be their house the very next day. So much was going through her head about the wedding, hoping everything worked out all right. She'd been in on the plans for many of her friends' weddings, but most of them hired a wedding planner or worked with the people at the venue to be sure everything came together right.

For Kate, the planning was done with just herself and the help of many of her friends. Her venue was the community center, which was just a building rented out for different events that didn't come with anyone to help plan them. It was her second wedding, and though it was no less important than her first, she felt like going all-out with a wedding planner wasn't quite right for them. She wanted it to be a fun, family gathering, which of course most weddings were, but making it more casual meant her details were a lot different than some other brides.

They'd planned on tables for kids' activities and kept the decorations simple and fun, which included a lot of balloons thanks to input from Holly and Cooper.

She stepped out of her car while Holly had already jumped out and ran for Cooper.

"My grandparents are coming!" Holly announced.

"Cool! Dad said we're getting them from the airport," Cooper responded.

"Yep! You're coming with us," Holly confirmed.

"I know!"

Kate chuckled as she approached Paul. "Hello."

Paul gave her a light kiss on the cheek. "Hi! Are you two ready to go?"

"We're ready," she confirmed.

They piled into Paul's large SUV that sat six people and headed toward the airport, stopping at a drive-thru to pick up some smoothies for the drive into the city.

"Be sure you don't spill anything," Kate warned, turning her head toward the seats behind her. "I don't want you to be messy when you see Grandma and Grandpa."

"Okay," Paul answered, and she turned to him and laughed.

"Well, I guess that goes for you, too," she said.

"I want to make a good impression," he said. "It's only the second time I've seen them in person."

"Well, you already did make quite an impression," she replied. "Dad talked endlessly about your phone call. It was really sweet of you to ask him that way."

"Of course," Paul said. "I would have visited him in person to ask if I could have."

"What'd you ask him?" Cooper asked.

"Silly. He had to ask Grandpa if he could marry Mom," Holly explained.

Kate turned back again in time to see Cooper with his eyes wide. "What? You mean I still have to ask parents to do stuff when I'm a grownup?"

"For that, yes," his father answered with a chuckle. He turned to

Kate, and they both laughed as she took another sip of her strawberry smoothie.

They arrived at the airport and found a parking space about a half hour before her parents were going to arrive. She was so happy they were making it to the wedding. She'd been worried since her mother was too sick with the flu to make the trip for her bridal shower, and she thought her father might get sick after that. But he didn't, and now she was going to see both of them very soon.

Holly ran up to them when they finally appeared in the disembarking crowd. "Grandma! Grandpa! You're here!"

"Yes, we are!" Kate's mother, Felicity, called out as she wrapped her arms around her granddaughter. "Oh, you're getting too big too fast. And now you're going to be a bridesmaid for your mother!"

Holly pulled back and was practically bouncing up and down with excitement. "Yes! Wait until you see my dress. It's awesome! Such a pretty blue, and it looks like a princess dress."

"I bet you look just like a princess," Felicity said. She looked up at Kate and pulled her in for a hug. "Oh, I'm so glad to be here for your wedding."

"I'm glad you're here," Kate said, returning the hug. "I was worried when you were sick before."

"Oh, that was nothing," Felicity insisted. "I was better within a week."

Before Kate could answer, her father, Justus, was giving her a hug. "It's so good to see you, kiddo."

She had to laugh at the nickname, which she supposed she'd never outgrow. She felt the same way about her own daughter, after all. She would always be her little girl, no matter how big she got. "Good to see you, Dad."

Paul greeted them both. "It's good to see you again." They'd visited last Christmas and brought presents for everyone, including Cooper, whom Felicity was hugging now.

"Oh, this is all so wonderful," she said.

"Let's go get your bags," Paul suggested.

Cooper and Holly helped take the bags off the conveyor belt as

Felicity and Justus pointed them out. After a light lunch in the food court, they were back on the road headed to Charles Town.

They went to Kate's house where Felicity and Justus would be staying for the wedding and for a couple of days afterward until Kate, Paul, Holly, and Cooper left for their family vacation, which they were taking instead of a traditional honeymoon. She and Paul had talked it over and decided they should all celebrate their first weeks as a family together. For the wedding night, Holly was staying with her grandparents while Cooper stayed with Casey and Isabelle next door.

They all sat in the living room after Paul and Cooper brought in their bags.

"So, are you excited about Disney World?" Felicity asked Holly.

"You bet! It's going to be so much fun!"

Everyone was excited as Kate and Paul described their plans for the trip to Florida. Eventually, the conversation turned back to the wedding.

"I'm going to enjoy walking you down the aisle," Justus said. "It's something us fathers love to do."

"I can't wait," Kate agreed.

"I can't wait to see the venue all decorated for your wedding," Felicity said.

Kate nodded. "Yes, our friends are working on it today. We set up the tables, and they insisted on decorating for us, so it's going to be a surprise to me, too."

"What are your colors again? Blue?" Felicity asked.

Kate nodded again. "Yes, that's right. We're doing different shades of blue since my dress is light blue, and the ladies will all be in ice blue. We'll have darker and lighter shades in the decorations, mixed with silver."

Felicity looked at her with a furrowed brow. "I'm sorry, did you say your dress is blue?"

Kate felt her smile drop. "Yes, it's light blue." She realized she'd never told her mother much about the dress, other than that she was having one made.

"Oh."

"Um, does everyone want something to drink?" Kate asked. "I have some tea or hot cocoa." Everyone said what they wanted, and she stood. "Mother, care to help in the kitchen?"

"Yes."

It was another one-word answer, and Kate knew she'd hear a lot more once she got into the kitchen, but she decided to make it a private conversation. She stole a quick glance toward Paul that she hoped gave him the hint.

"So, Justus, tell me about that new woodworking saw you got for Christmas," Paul said as Kate and her mother left the room.

He got it, she thought.

Safely in the kitchen, she turned to her mother. "Mom, I've been married before, and I'm a mother. I can't wear a white dress."

"I suppose not, but light blue?" Felicity said. "I just don't think that's right for you. Why didn't you go with off-white?"

"I wanted it to be blue," Kate insisted.

"I just think the off-white would be more elegant for your age," her mother argued. "Light blue sounds like a child's dress.

Kate exhaled slowly. There was only one way to convince her mother and get the subject dropped. "Okay, Mom, let's get everyone their drinks but hold off on ours. I want to show you something."

Felicity shrugged. "Okay. But I still think I'm right."

Kate held her tongue as they made all the cocoa, which everyone seemed to prefer, and they both carried the mugs to the living room.

"Everyone, I just remembered an errand I have to do, and Mom's going with me," Kate said. She wanted to pull Paul aside to explain, but from the look in his eyes, she didn't have to.

"No problem," he said. "Justus was just telling me about the planter boxes he built. I'll stay here with him and the children until you get back."

"Thank you," she said, but she mouthed an extra "thank you" as he handed her the keys to the SUV, since her car was at his house.

She texted Penny, who was thankfully at the bridal shop and answered quickly, and drove her mother to the store.

"I want you to see this firsthand," she explained. "I had my dress custom made by an amazing seamstress who makes nothing but wedding dresses and bridesmaid's dresses. She's an incredible talent."

"All right," her mother said as they otherwise drove in silence to the shop.

"Kate!" Penny greeted her when they walked into the shop. "Oh, this must be your mother. Felicity, right? You two look so much alike." She looked directly at Felicity. "Kate has your eyes."

Felicity nodded and greeted her politely, but not as warmly as she normally would. Kate knew she was upset because she was still sure she was right.

"I have your dress hanging in the fitting room," Penny said. "Please, take all the time you need."

"Thank you," Kate said, leading her mother to the room. "You can have a seat, Mom." She took the garment bag off the rack and carried it behind the privacy screen. She put it on as much as she could without help finishing the zipping and stepped out.

"This is it," she said. "It's a beautiful dress, handmade by a wonderful church-going woman who makes these just for the joy of seeing women start their happy lives with the men they love."

Her mother remained in her chair without saying a word.

Kate walked over to another garment bag Penny had put there and took out an off-white dress, holding it up in front of her. "This is how this color looks on me. It's drab and dull against my hair color."

Again, her mother was silent.

She put the off-white dress back on the rack and turned to face her mother. "Yes, I wore a white dress once," she continued. "I thought it would be my one and only wedding. All I wanted then was to spend the rest of my life with Vaughn. And then we had Holly, the greatest gift God could give a woman. And then we lost him, our husband and father. I thought I'd never be happy again. I didn't know how I was going to make it one day to the next, much less be happy."

She swallowed, feeling the lump in her throat as tears started to well in her eyes. "Then Paul came along. He's a wonderful man who loves God and loves me and your granddaughter. He makes us both happy and completes the family I started with Vaughn, and—"

Her mother put her hand up to stop her. "Just… stop. Stop right there."

Kate readied herself to argue as her mother stood and walked up to her. Felicity's voice softened. "This is the most beautiful dress I've ever seen, and you look like an angel in it."

"Mom—"

Felicity put up her hand again. "I don't know why I ever doubt any of your choices. You are a wise woman who thinks things through, and you make all your choices with God in the forefront of your mind and love in your heart."

Kate swallowed again, trying not to cry.

"Whoever this dressmaker is," Felicity continued, touching the lacy fabric delicately, "she's so very talented. She's captured not only your outer beauty, but the beauty inside you. You know what it's like to be a mother. Everything worries me. Sweetie, I'm so sorry I ever doubted you. I guess, half the time, I'm doubting myself. I want everything in your life to be perfect. You're a wonderful daughter. I love you so much, and I can't wait to see you get married in this… oh, my goodness, this stunning blue dress."

She reached out her arms, and Kate nearly dove into them, wrapping her mother in a tight hug as tears rolled down her cheeks. "I love you, Mom," she said.

Felicity squeezed her tighter. "I love you, my baby girl." She pulled back, and her face was dripping with tears as well. "Now, let's go get ready for this wedding. I hear we have a rehearsal tonight."

CHAPTER TEN

"Oh, that's beautiful." Isabelle ran her finger gently over the dark blue ribbon of the centerpiece.

"Thanks," Macey said. "I wanted something a little different for the rehearsal dinner table. I'll bring the regular ones when we set up tomorrow morning."

They both jumped a little at a popping sound and turned to look at the other side of the community center hall.

Sam shrugged as he picked up the popped balloon and threw it away. "Sorry. Got carried away on that one."

"You're having too much fun with the balloon machine, my dear husband," Macey said, her expression half serious and half laughing.

Isabelle thought it was hilarious. He'd been blowing up so many balloons, she wasn't sure how they were going to get them all hung in time for the rehearsal.

"Anyway," Macey said, adjusting the centerpiece one more time. "Let's go make sure the altar looks good."

Isabelle nodded, and they went into the connecting room where the ceremony would be held. There weren't any balloons there, just beautiful ribbons and flowers lining the rows of chairs.

"I didn't bring everything for this yet," Macey explained. "The ones directly around the altar platform are a lot more delicate, so I'll set them up last thing in the morning."

"Kate is going to love this," Isabelle said. "I love it. With more flowers tomorrow, it'll be even more stunning." She was so happy for her friend and soon-to-be sister-in-law. They'd grown a lot closer in recent years as they both dated brothers and ended up on a lot of double dates. She was so thrilled to be her matron of honor, and it was going to be a lot of fun walking back down an aisle with her husband Casey again.

Macey nodded. "I love this mix of blues. I don't get to do that style very often. Most people want pinks and reds lately for their weddings."

"It's very nice."

"We'd better help Sam get those balloons up before everyone gets here," Macey said.

"Yes," Isabelle agreed. "We only have an hour before the rest of the guests show up."

They went back out to the main hall where Sam was already hanging balloons.

Macey laughed. "I thought you'd still be blowing up more of them."

He turned to her and chuckled. "I ran out. I guess that means it's time to get them hung."

"Exactly."

Isabelle laughed at their banter and started helping them fasten the balloons wherever the decorative ribbons met on the walls and corners of tables. She turned when cold air rushed in with the front door opening and closing.

"I got it!" Casey announced. "The print shop apologized for being so late. They had a lot of rush orders and had to work most of the day to get everything done."

"I'm sorry they had to work today," Isabelle said. "Everyone should get the week after Christmas off. But I'm glad they got the banner finished. I was hoping we'd have it up tonight."

"It's pretty big," Casey said. "But I think it'll work perfectly."

Sam got off the step stool and headed for the closet. "I'll get out the bigger ladder for that."

"We'll keep hanging balloons in these lower spots," Macey suggested, and she and Isabelle took over the stepladder duty.

The men hung the banner, along with a few balloons on its edges, and they all stepped back to admire the decorations.

"'Congratulations, Paul and Kate.' That's perfect," Isabelle said.

Macey nodded. "They did a nice job on that. It matches the colors well."

"All right, we're good to go." Casey said it just as the cold air whooshed in again as the catering team arrived.

Isabelle ran up to greet them. "Hello, Grace. You have perfect timing."

"Hello, Isabelle, and I'm glad." Grace chuckled. She turned and directed her team to the community center kitchen so they could get the food prepared.

"Thank you for doing this today and on New Year's Eve," Isabelle added.

"Not a problem," Grace said. "Kate and Paul are part of our congregation, so they're family. Besides, I'm looking forward to the wedding. It looks like a party in here."

Isabelle laughed, looking around at all the balloons and ribbons everywhere, as well as the giant banner. "I guess it does. It will be fun. Your kids will love the activities we have planned. Kate wanted it to be fun for the whole family."

"I can't wait." Grace gestured toward the kitchen with a nod. "We should have everything heated and ready in a half hour."

"Perfect. Thank you again."

Isabelle, Casey, Macey, and Sam put away the balloon equipment and ladders and made sure all the chairs were set and ready for the rehearsal dinner. Casey left to pick up his mother, Shirley, and a few minutes later, everyone started arriving.

"Oh, my goodness," Kate said when she walked in. "It looks incredible in here." She gave Isabelle and Macey hugs. "Thank you so much."

She turned to Casey, who had just returned with Shirley, and Sam, but Paul was already thanking them. "This is perfect," he said. "Thank you."

"Wow!"

Isabelle turned to see Cooper, who was looking around in awe at all the balloons. "This is so cool!"

She let out a chuckle. "I'm glad you like it, Cooper."

"It's real neat, Mrs. Abernathy," he said.

"I love it too," Holly agreed. "Grandma, look at the balloons!"

"My, those are lovely," Felicity said. "It looks very festive in here."

The door opened again for Olivia and Memphis to enter. "Oh, this looks fun!" Olivia said.

Similar expressions of appreciation continued as Erin and Luke, then Melody, Reid, and their son arrived, along with Mrs. Gregory, the sweet white-haired woman everyone adored. Since Casey was busy as best man for this wedding, she would play the piano as Melody sang their song, Natalie Cole's version of *The Very Thought of You*.

Melody and Reid's son, Michael, ran up to Holly and Cooper and started chatting excitedly. The three were best friends, and Isabelle knew they spent a lot of time together.

"Where's Sadie?" she asked.

Melody turned her gaze from her son to Isabelle. "My mom's watching her. We'll bring her for the wedding tomorrow."

They turned toward the door again as Pastor Lloyd arrived and greeted everyone with a wide smile. "Well, there certainly are a lot of joyous occasions this season. I'm so thrilled to officiate another wedding."

Paul shook his hand. "Thank you so much for coming." He took the pastor's coat and hung it by the door. "I think we're all here and ready to start, if you're ready."

"I am," Pastor Lloyd said. "Groom and groomsmen, come with me.

Bridal party, you'll enter through the door when we're ready. Do we have someone who can seat the parents?"

Memphis raised his hand. "That'll be me."

"Perfect. Let's get started." The pastor went into the room set up for the ceremony.

Paul gave Kate a quick kiss before he followed, along with his brother and the other groomsmen, which included Cooper.

"I have piano duty," Mrs. Gregory happily announced, and she followed them into the room, where they'd already set up the upright piano the community center had in one of the storage closets.

Memphis sat Sam and Macey, who Kate had asked to stay for the rehearsal and dinner, as well as his wife first, then he escorted Shirley and then Felicity to their seats to the quiet music of Mrs. Gregory's piano.

"Okay, Holly, your turn," Isabelle said.

Kate's daughter nodded and walked into the room and slowly up the aisle.

"She's getting good at this," Isabelle noted.

Kate nodded. "She's been in a few weddings now, first as a flower girl and now as a bridesmaid. She really does love it."

"My turn," Erin said when Holly got halfway.

Isabelle waited and soon left Kate and her father, turning when she finally reached the altar and took her place, looking up to catch Casey's eye. He winked at her, and she had to hold in a giggle.

Kate looked so happy walking up the aisle with her father. Isabelle almost had a tear fall, knowing how much Kate and Paul had been through before finally having this second chance at happiness. She couldn't imagine losing Casey, and to have that happen after having a child together was unthinkable. She knew Paul never even had a chance to say goodbye to his wife Tanya before she succumbed to her illness since he'd been out of town. Poor Cooper and Holly had each been left without one of their parents.

But now, looking at all of their smiles, Isabelle knew she was witnessing one of the miracles God brought to this life. From such tragedy, they'd found love and family for a second chance.

The pastor said an opening prayer and a few words, explaining he'd skip some of the service in the interest of time. But Melody sang their song beautifully, and Olivia recited a portion of her Bible verses, which were lovely. They both had such beautiful voices, Isabelle thought.

Then it was time for the vows, which Isabelle knew would be so beautiful, and even though they didn't recite them during the rehearsal, she nearly cried again but managed to hold back her tears. They all applauded when Pastor Lloyd said it was where he would pronounce them man and wife.

"But I'm not going to do that yet," he said with a chuckle.

Everyone laughed as they all went back down the aisle into the main hall, where they took their seats for dinner. This time, Pastor Lloyd had agreed to stay and eat.

"You caught me at a good time," he said. "Usually, I need to run off for something, but tonight, I have the time." The caterer's assistant placed his plate in front of him. "And this looks delicious, thank you."

"That's why we're here," Sam joked.

Everyone laughed, including the pastor, and Macey just shook her head, but Isabelle could see the smile trying to burst out of her friend. Sam was always so much fun to be around.

"Would you do us the honor of saying grace, Pastor Lloyd?" Paul asked.

"I'd love to." The pastor said a few beautiful words of thanks before closing the prayer.

"Amen," Isabelle said with the others.

They all started eating, and the room was quiet for a moment as they enjoyed the food.

"Melody, your singing is amazing," Isabelle said after a while.

"Oh, yes, it definitely is," Felicity agreed. "And you're quite talented on the piano, Patricia."

Isabelle was surprised to hear Mrs. Gregory being called by her first name, but she'd noticed she and Kate's mother had been chatting in the corner for a while before the dinner. Mrs. Gregory thanked her with a smile.

"I guess ours is the last wedding between our group of friends," Kate said. "I really think it'll be wonderful to start off the new year with all of us married couples."

Felicity nodded. "It was so much fun for me and Justus when all our friends were finally married. It brings the friendships to a whole new level as you experience the next stages of life together."

"Well said," Mrs. Gregory agreed. "And many of you are already starting families. That's the next step, you know," she said with a wink toward Kate. "Well, you will have a built-in family, won't you?"

"We will." Kate nodded. "But we'd love to expand it, if God decides to bless us in that way. I can't really ask for more with how wonderful things are for us now."

Mrs. Gregory smiled. "I'm sure He has plenty of plans for your future."

Kate smiled.

"This dinner is wonderful," Justus said.

Paul nodded, finishing his bite. "It is. Grace and her crew do a fantastic job. They're catering the wedding tomorrow, too."

"Well, one more reason not to miss it." Justus chuckled.

"Dad, you're not going to miss it anyway," Kate said. "You've got a job to do. Remember that."

"Oh, I'll make sure he's there on time," Felicity said. "Don't worry about that."

"I'm kidding, kiddo," Justus said. "You know I wouldn't miss this for the world. It's a father's greatest duty to walk his daughter down the aisle."

Kate smiled, and Isabelle saw the happiness in her eyes. She was so excited for her friend and her beautiful wedding tomorrow.

CHAPTER ELEVEN

KATE

KATE REACHED OVER TO SHUT OFF THE ALARM ON HER PHONE. SHE FELT like she'd only gotten a few hours of sleep, and she figured that was probably accurate. She'd fallen asleep fairly quickly by the time they'd gotten home from the rehearsal dinner and had chatted with her parents in the living room for a long time while they drank hot cocoa. But throughout the night, she kept waking up, and every time she did, it was harder to get back to sleep.

She threw off her covers and got dressed, heading to the bathroom mirror to brush out her auburn hair and tie it back. She avoided makeup so the makeup artist, Gloria, could start with a clean slate later, and Valerie would be doing her magic to her hair, so she didn't need to bother with it for once.

Looking into the mirror, her smile grew. This was her wedding day, again. She remembered her thoughts on her first wedding day so long ago. She'd been a nervous wreck, so excited about finally marrying Vaughn and so worried something would go wrong. She worried the cake would melt or she'd forget her vows, though her biggest fear at the time was that she'd trip on her dress and fall flat on her face in front of everyone.

How unimportant all those things seemed now—had she known she would lose him in just a few short years, maybe she would have paid more attention to enjoying the day and not stressing out about the little details that no one would have really minded. She was different now—a mother, a widow, and now, a bride again.

She smiled, determined to truly enjoy this day.

That enjoyment started when she left her room as the scent of a very familiar breakfast wafted through the air. She went straight to the kitchen.

"Mom, you didn't need to go through all that trouble."

Her mother didn't even turn to face her, flipping the pancakes in the pan in front of her. "Of course, I did," she said. "It's your wedding day. You shouldn't have to cook breakfast."

"And you knew I'd love your banana pancakes." She put one arm around her mother and gave her a hug. "Thank you."

"You're welcome." With both hands busy, Felicity leaned her head against her quickly in return. "Now, go sit in the dining room with your dad and your daughter. You don't have to do any work today. We'll take care of it all."

Knowing it would be useless to argue, she thanked her again and went to go see the others.

"It's your wedding day!" Holly said as soon as she walked into the dining room. "It's so exciting!"

"It is," Kate agreed, pulling out her chair and sitting near her father. "Good morning, Dad. Good morning, Holly."

"Good morning," they both answered at once, and Holly giggled.

"Your mother insisted that we sit here and wait for our banana pancakes," Justus said. "I'm not inclined to argue."

Kate laughed. "Fair enough. But Holly, I'll need you to help Grandma clean up."

"I already told her I would," Holly said. "Grandma just wanted to do the cooking alone."

Kate nodded and smiled. Soon, Felicity came in with a huge stack of pancakes along with some bacon. Justus said grace, and they all split the pancakes, which Kate had to admit were a few more than she probably should have eaten, but her mother's banana pancakes were so good.

Again, she remembered her first wedding, when she could barely eat a bite because her stomach was tied up in knots. She'd taken a few bites of dry toast, and that was all she could handle before the ceremony was over and lunch was served.

But today, she was going to enjoy every minute of it, including the delicious breakfast.

"Mom, I can help," she tried to insist after they'd finished and Felicity rose to gather the plates.

"Not today, you can't," Felicity said. "Holly and I have this all under control."

"I guess you're stuck with me, kiddo," her father said.

She laughed. "I guess so." She watched as her mother and daughter cleared the plates and left the room.

"She's been planning this for a while."

Kate turned to look at her father.

"She wanted you to have a really good day after—" He paused. "Well, after your last wedding. I'm sorry for bringing it up."

"It's okay, Dad," she said. "It still hurts that I lost Vaughn. But Paul and Cooper are so wonderful. I'm happy. And now, I can look back at things as fond memories without my heart shattering."

"That's good to hear," he said. "Your mother and I worry about you."

"You don't have to anymore," she insisted. "I have Paul, and I'm going to be very busy with this instant family."

Justus smiled. "That's a wonderful thing. I just hope I don't trip over your dress."

"Daddy—" She started to chastise him, but she saw he was teasing. She'd explained later after her first wedding how worried she was about tripping in front of everyone.

Holly still had a lot of energy left after cleaning the kitchen, and it was hard to get her to be patient.

"Can't we go now?" she'd asked several times. "We could get dressed early just so we're ready."

"It's way too early," Kate insisted. "Don't worry. We'll leave soon."

After a morning of reminiscing, her mother made a light lunch, again insisting on doing it alone, and after that was cleaned up—by Holly and Felicity alone again—they sat and chatted for a bit before it was time for Holly and Kate to leave.

"Do you have everything?" Justus asked after helping load a few things into the car. The dress was already waiting in the changing room at the community center, so there wasn't much to remember.

Kate nodded. "I think so."

"We'll see you there, sweetheart," Felicity said, hugging her daughter. "I'll come see you as soon as I get there."

"See you there." Kate and Holly got buckled in, and she took a deep breath before driving them both to the community center. She checked her phone before going in to be sure Paul hadn't arrived yet, but Isabelle assured her that he hadn't, and that he was waiting until she was there and safely in the changing room so he wouldn't see her before the wedding.

She stepped inside and got into the room to see that Valerie and Gloria had already arrived and were setting up their tools.

"I'm giving you to Gloria first," Valerie said. "Then I'll do your hair. In the meantime, Isabelle, you're up!"

Isabelle plopped into the chair while Valerie started on her hair, and Gloria took a few things out of her makeup bag before starting on her. Kate wasn't crazy about wearing much makeup, but she knew from her first wedding that some was required so the pictures turned out well.

She truly treasured those pictures now.

Keeping as still as possible for the makeup, she watched Valerie transform Isabelle's lovely blonde hair into strands of bouncy curls, tying it up in some places to let the hair underneath, which had even more natural curl, shine through. It was beautiful, and her almost sister-in-law was going to look stunning in her ice blue dress.

Erin arrived when Kate's makeup was done, and she slipped into the spot for Gloria to finish up, so she watched as Valerie made Kate's co-worker's strawberry blonde hair look stunning as well. They all chatted as Valerie finished with her and switched to Holly, who was clearly enjoying her pampering treatment.

"You and Cooper are going to look so nice," Isabelle said. "So, he'll be carrying the rings even though he's a groomsman now and no longer a ring bearer, right?"

A lump instantly formed in Kate's stomach as panic washed over her. "Oh, no. I didn't get the rings!"

Isabelle turned to her, wide-eyed at first but then clearly putting on her calm teacher's expression. "Okay, don't panic. It'll be okay. Are they at your house? Are your parents still there?"

Kate nodded. "Yes. Holly, hand me my phone." Her daughter did so quickly, and she called her mother. "Mom, I forgot the rings."

"Kate?" her mom said on the call. "We've already left."

"Oh, no!"

"Kate, don't panic," Felicity said. "Your father and I can turn around. We're not far from there."

"Okay." Kate tried to take a calming breath. "They're in my bedroom in the top drawer of my vanity."

"Okay, sweetie," her mother said. "Don't worry. I'll call you when we get them."

She hung up and looked up at Isabelle, still feeling the panic.

"It's okay," Isabelle said.

"Yes, it'll be fine." Erin had switched on her counselor's mode. "We have plenty of time for them to get them and get here in time."

Kate nodded, feeling silly for acting like a first-time bride once again, though she knew she'd still be nervous until her parents arrived with the rings.

"I forgot too, Mom," Holly said. "I'm sorry."

Kate put a smile on her face, glad she could use her mothering skills to take the focus off her own panic. "It's okay. It's not your job to remember. We both forgot, and that's okay. Grandma and Grandpa will bring them." She gave Holly a hug to reassure her. "Your hair looks so pretty. Why don't you get your dress on? By the time they get here, it'll be almost time for the wedding."

"Okay!"

She sat for her hair styling and felt calmer after reassuring Holly, at least until her phone rang. "Mom?"

"They're not there," her mother said.

"What?" The panic returned. "I had them in the first drawer."

"Let me look again. I'll put you on speaker."

Kate found herself tapping her foot as she waited, searching her mind trying to remember if she'd moved the rings. She didn't think she had, but things had been busy lately. She felt like her heart was pounding its way out of her chest.

"Nothing," her mother said, and Kate's panic returned.

"You're trying the top drawer?" she asked.

"Yes, dear," Felicity confirmed. "I pulled on the knob, and there's nothing here but some perfumes and powder makeup."

"Oh." Kate exhaled. "That's the left drawer. Try the right one."

"The right?"

"Yes, it doesn't have a knob," Kate explained. "It's one of those that you pull from the top."

"I see it," she heard her father say in the background, hearing the drawer pull open as well.

"Oh, here they are!" her mother exclaimed. "They're in the black ring boxes, right?"

"That's them!" She put her hand over her chest as relief washed over her. "Thank you Mom and Dad."

"Yay!" Holly exclaimed with a big smile that made Kate feel a bit better.

She said goodbye to her parents and leaned back in her chair. "That was close. Oh, no. What if I forgot something else?"

Isabelle laughed. "I don't think you did. And if you did, we'll improvise. With all the weddings we've been having over the last couple of years, all of us are pretty good at this."

Kate let out a chuckle, her heart finally calming. "That's true. We should open a wedding planning business."

"Maybe we should," Erin agreed, laughing.

"I just can't believe I forgot something that important when I've done this before," Kate said.

Isabelle shook her head. "It's a big day! It's easy to forget things. Don't worry."

Soon, her parents arrived, and her mother came in after Kate and the bridesmaids were dressed. "Your father took the rings straight to Paul," she said.

"Thank you so much."

"Oh, you look so stunning," her mother said. "Holly, maybe you'd like to wear this beautiful dress at your wedding."

"What?" Holly's eyes went wide before she shook her head vigorously. "Nope, I'm not doing this. Boys are gross!"

Kate and everyone else in the room giggled, but she couldn't wait to see her little girl walk down the aisle one day and start a new life with the perfect man for her.

Isabelle got a text. "We're ready to go! We'll see you there."

Kate gave Holly a hug before she stepped out to follow Isabelle and Erin out the door. She turned to the mirror and took a breath as her mother came up behind her. "You look so beautiful."

"That she does."

They turned to see Justus coming through the door. "I think they're waiting on you, Felicity."

Her mother nodded and gave Kate a tight hug. "I'll see you soon, sweetie."

"See you, Mom." Kate turned to her father as her mother walked out the door.

"Well, we've been in this situation before, haven't we?" He chuckled. "That means I'm really good at this."

She laughed with him. "I suppose you are."

" I've already given you the father speech," he continued. "I guess there's not much to say except, I'm proud of you, Kate. Paul is a good man, I'm so excited to see the two of you grow stronger as a couple led by the Lord. Now, let's get you married."

He held out his elbow, and she wrapped her arm around his. "Let's go."

CHAPTER TWELVE

WHAT A DIFFERENCE IT WAS FOR PAUL, STANDING AT THE ALTAR WAITING for his bride to walk down the aisle, compared to the first time he'd done it. He mused about how he had been such a younger man then, not just in age but in maturity and life experience.

He remembered being so nervous he could barely stand in one place. His brother Casey stood beside him then, too, whispering in his ear to relax to reassure him he wouldn't mess up his vows or faint and fall over. Of course, between brothers, communication was, more often than not, done using a teasing code gleaned from years of shared experiences, and this was no different.

Paul remembered the exact words Casey had told him. "Get a grip."

It worked well enough because he'd gotten through the ceremony without messing up once.

But today, Paul stood in one spot, calm and content with only happiness in his heart. He knew God had brought him straight to

Kate when he needed to climb up from a deep well of darkness. When Tonya first passed away, it seemed like all the love had been sucked from the earth. Even though their son Cooper was still there and needed him more than ever, he couldn't seem to get past the over-whelming ache in his heart that festered there so long after she was gone.

Casey and his mother held things together for Cooper as much as they could, and for that, he was so grateful. And then God led him to Kate, who showed him just how much love was left in the world and that it was endless.

In the middle of his thoughts, the piano music changed, and there she was, standing in the doorway on her father's arm. He hitched his breath because, from that distance, she looked like an angel in the soft, billowing fabric in the lightest shade of blue, her beautiful auburn hair flowing behind her and accented with a cascade of light blue and white flowers in place of a traditional veil. He could barely breathe, until he heard his brother's voice whisper from beside him.

"Get a grip."

This time, there was a chuckle that followed, and he would have laughed, too, if he weren't still mesmerized by the woman walking down the aisle. Finally, she was standing right in front of him.

"Who gives this woman in marriage?" Pastor Lloyd asked.

"Her mother and I do." Justus gave his daughter a kiss on the cheek and put her hand in Paul's, and they turned to face the pastor who began the opening prayer.

It was hard to take his eyes off Kate, but he bowed his head and squeezed her hand, and Pastor Lloyd thanked God for His guidance and blessings on their marriage. Paul said a grateful "Amen" at the end, along with everyone else.

Then the pastor gave a brief sermon about marriage, love, and family. He knew Paul and Kate well, so Paul knew Pastor Lloyd was aware of their circumstances and that an instant family would be formed when he declared them man and wife. So, he spoke in length about how that family could bond together stronger as the years went on. Finally, he gestured toward the side of the room, and the piano music started again, with Mrs. Gregory handling the keys gracefully.

This time, Melody started singing their song, *The Very Thought of You*, in her soft, melodic voice that carried well in the large community center room. He and Kate turned toward her, their hands still grasping each other tightly as they listened to the beautiful song that spoke so truthfully of the feelings he had right at that moment.

When the music stopped, Olivia took Melody's place on the elevated platform and began speaking. "Today, we're celebrating the love of Paul and Kate. There are things unique and beautiful about every wedding, but for these two, one thing that stands out is how God's compassion worked to bring them together from a past full of heartache. The Bible celebrates this in Lamentations 3:21-23, and I'd like to remind you all of this today."

She went on to read the passage, which Paul realized was very fitting for their special day, and she followed it up with thoughtful wishes and warm words of friendship explaining her choice. She read some other passages, ones Paul knew well, some he'd heard at other weddings and some he had not, then she put away her notes and nodded at the pastor before stepping down.

"Paul and Kate have chosen some words of their own to share today," Pastor Lloyd said. "Kate, Paul, know that these promises you make before God and these loved ones gathered here today will be the ones you fall back on in times ahead, whether those are joyful or troubling. Paul, if you'll begin, please."

Paul nodded, clearing his throat as quietly as he could before he began. He turned to Kate and took both her hands in his. "Kate, it's hard to put into words what you mean to me. But since you and I have lived a similar path, I know that much of what I say will reach your ears but be interpreted through your heart. I wound up in a dark, cold place before, and I didn't know how to get out, or even whether I had it in me to dig my way out if I saw a beam of light. But then you came, and your light was so strong, entwined with God's love because He brought me to you, and together, you both brought me to the world of sunshine and laughter again. Now, I never want to leave your side. Knowing where I'd been and how that felt, I thought carefully of the promises I wanted to make to you today. It kept coming back to love. I promise that I will always love you, and just those words mean so much more—that I'll respect you and honor you, listen to you and truly hear you, and comfort you and soothe you when that's needed. I'll encourage you and support you, find all the ways I can to bring more joy to your life, and I'll always keep your love close to my heart, no matter what I do. There's one thing I can't promise—that I'll never feel darkness again. But if I do, I can promise that it will be your love and God's love that I turn to first to bring me out of it and into your arms. I love you, Kate."

He exhaled, happy that he'd said everything that was in his heart.

"Kate," the pastor said, nodding toward her.

"Paul," she began, her eyes moist and glistening. "I charged straight forward in life, trying to hold things together when my heart was shattered. I visited that dark place where you lived for so long, and it took everything in my heart and all the love of God to keep me from completely falling apart. For so long, I survived but didn't think much about really living. But from our first dance, your light sparked in my heart. Every day, I grow more excited about the future, and I feel more alive than I've ever felt before. We're about to make a whole, complete family once these vows are finished, and I couldn't ask for a happier life. We will both be truly living again. So, I promise to keep my love for you at the forefront of my heart, to honor you, respect you, and be there for you in every way. I love you so much, Paul."

Her eyes sparkled so much as she said the words, he almost didn't hear the pastor until he said his name again in a very important question.

"Paul Bryant, do you take Kate Woods to be your lawfully wedded wife, to have and to hold from this day forward, for better or for worse, for richer or for poorer, in sickness and in health, and will you love, honor, and cherish her for as long as you both shall live?"

"I do," he said quickly.

Kate smiled, and the pastor spoke again. "Kate Woods, do you take this man, Paul Bryant, to be your lawfully wedded husband, to have and to hold from this day forward, for better or for worse, for richer or for poorer, in sickness and in health, and will you love, honor, and cherish him for as long as you both shall live?"

"I do," Kate said with a smile, and his heart skipped a beat.

"The rings please," Pastor Lloyd said.

Paul watched as his brother handed the rings to the pastor, and he in turn gave Kate's ring to him.

"Repeat after me," the pastor said. "With this ring, I thee wed."

"With this ring, I thee wed," Paul said, sliding it carefully onto her finger. When he looked up, her eyes twinkled while the pastor handed her his ring.

"With this ring, I thee wed," the pastor repeated.

Kate's smile grew wider. "With this ring, I thee wed."

Pastor Lloyd continued. "Paul and Kate, you have both proclaimed your love for one another and your commitment to honor and cherish each other for life, in the sight of Almighty God and in front of these witnesses. There's just one more thing for me to say. By the power vested in me by the Church and the state of West Virginia, I pronounce you husband and wife. Paul, you may kiss your bride."

He wrapped both arms around his new wife and kissed her softly, barely aware of the cheers and applause that was happening all around them. He didn't want to, but he knew he had to pull back to finish the ceremony and get on with the reception, so he did, grasping her hand firmly as they made their way back down the aisle.

Olivia and Memphis had already started arranging everyone in a receiving line that led from the ceremony room to the main hall, so as they passed through, they greeted friends and family who were showering them with congratulations.

Melanie and Reid were at the front of the line, with Michael beside them holding Sadie's hand. "What a beautiful ceremony," Melody said. "Congratulations."

"You made it even more beautiful with your stunning voice," Kate said while hugging her.

"It was my honor to sing your song," Melody insisted.

They continued through the line as he shook hands and received a few hugs as they went. Though he loved sharing the day with his friends and family, he was craving a moment alone with his wife just as they reached the end of the line, where Isabelle steered them into a small room off the main hall.

"I'll knock when it's time for pictures," she said, shutting the door behind them.

He looked at Kate, hardly believing everything that had just happened. They were married. She was his wife now, and their family was complete. He gave her a deeper kiss than he'd felt comfortable doing in front of the pastor and their children, then just held her closely.

"We did it!" she said.

He pulled back a little so he could look into her eyes. "Yes, we did. And I didn't even mess up my lines." They both chuckled.

"Me, neither," she said. "I think being older and being through… everything, helped me enjoy the day more."

"Same here," he agreed. "I got to really enjoy watching you walk down the aisle toward me. You look stunning."

She smiled. "Thanks. You look pretty good yourself."

"Thank you." He kissed her lightly again.

She looked down at her hand and moved her engagement ring back to her left finger, twisting it a little to get it flush against her wedding band, which fit in with the design. "I didn't get a chance to tell you. I forgot the rings, and my parents had to find them. And they couldn't find them!"

He chuckled. "Well, looks like it worked out just fine in the end."

She looked into his eyes. "Yes, it sure did."

They turned to a light knock on the door and heard Isabelle's voice. "Are you ready?"

"Yes," they both said at once, and they chuckled.

"Alec announced the appetizers, and Grace's team is on it!" Isabelle said. "The photographer wants us in the ceremony room for photos."

Kate, Paul, and their wedding party took a few minutes with the photographer, and Lexi walked around behind him getting shots for Sophie and Zach. Once they were finished, they walked down the small hallway as Alec announced them. "I'm happy to introduce Paul and Kate Bryant!"

CHAPTER THIRTEEN

Kate

The applause continued as they walked hand-in-hand up to the DJ station, where Alec handed Paul the microphone.

"Thank you, all of you," Paul said as the applause slowly quieted. "We're so blessed to have you all share this day with us, especially since it's New Year's Eve, and you may have other plans later, but we invite everyone who can to stay with us for our New Year's ball drop. It'll be spectacular, I promise." Light chuckles echoed through the crowd.

"We're doing a couple of things differently, as you can probably see by the tables over to the side there," he continued. "We'll be serving dinner first, and after that, we'll open the tables for craft projects for the children here today. We hope this makes the day fun for everyone. The moment Kate and I were married, we created an instant family. We wanted to celebrate the blessing of family with all of you. Also, Kate and I would like to thank Grace and her team for the fantastic meal you're about to receive." He gestured toward the buffet table, where Grace gave a smile and a wave. "But first, I'd like to ask if Pastor Lloyd would do us the honor of leading us in prayer."

The pastor rose and walked up to the microphone. "I'd be honored," he said. Everyone bowed their heads as he began. "Dear Lord, thank you for the blessing of witnessing the joining of these two wonderful people in Holy Matrimony. Thank you for the gathering here of their beloved friends and family to share in the event, and please watch over all of them as well as those who could not be here today. Thank you for the blessing of this food that we may break bread together as companions in service of You. Please bless all those who are in need today, and help us keep the grace of service toward them in our hearts at all times. In the name of our Savior Jesus Christ, we pray. Amen."

"Amen." Kate looked up as the pastor handed the microphone back to Paul, and he gave it to her. "All right, everyone," she said. "Please help yourselves to the wonderful buffet at the back of the room." Sounds of chairs moving and chatting echoed through the room as everyone made their way to the buffet line then waited for Paul and Kate to take the lead.

The server held her plate behind the impressive table in front of Kate, and she wasn't sure what she wanted to choose. They'd decided on a mix of simpler foods that children would enjoy as well as some dishes for more sophisticated tastes, with entrees of beef, chicken, and salmon with plenty of sides and snack foods. She went with the salmon and rice pilaf but couldn't resist a scoop of the macaroni and cheese just because it looked so good with the bread crumb topping.

"What?" she asked when Paul looked at her with a raised brow. "Admit it. You want a scoop, too."

"I do," he agreed.

She laughed as the server added it to his plate. "That's the second time you've said that today."

"I liked the first time best," he said. She smiled at him as they headed to their seats.

"Wait!"

Kate turned her head to see Lexi holding out her phone. "Okay, here's the bride and groom taking their first meal together back to their seats. Look at that salmon. Looks like a satisfying meal there if I've ever seen one."

Kate chuckled as she took her seat. "You're not missing a detail, are you?"

"Nope," Lexi said. "I promised Sophie I'd give her the play-by-play so she won't miss a thing."

"That's really sweet of you," Kate said. "But I don't think she'll have time to worry about what we're eating while she's on her fabulous honeymoon."

Lexi shrugged. "She can fast-forward it if she wants. But I bet she wants to see it." She followed them as they took their seats and then started her phone's camera again. "Here's the happy couple sitting at the head table. Aren't they adorable?"

Kate and Paul both laughed and leaned a little closer to pose for the video. "Hi, Sophie and Zach!" Kate waved. "I hope you're having an amazing honeymoon! We had a wonderful wedding!"

"Perfect," Lexi said, lowering her phone. "Oh, no. I didn't get a shot of the buffet yet. I'd better do that before it's empty. Have fun!"

"Have fun, Lexi," Kate said. She and Paul both chuckled as they started eating. "Mm, this is good."

"It is," he agreed.

She glanced over at Holly and Cooper who were at the end of the line for food since they'd spent time excitedly talking to Michael. "They sure are happy," she said.

"So are we." Paul smiled. "I think we have ourselves the perfect family."

"I agree." She took a bite of her dinner. "Oh, and I was right about the mac and cheese. It's just like my grandma used to make."

He laughed and gestured toward his plate. "It is delicious. That's why I ate all of it first."

They finished eating and watched as Isabelle, Max, Macey, and Sam got all the children started on art projects. Kate had noticed at other weddings that some children started to look bored when it came to all the standard wedding traditions like the dances. She'd talked it over with Paul, and they decided to have the crafts happening at the same time so those who wanted to dance or watch the dancing could do so while others did crafts. Plus, keeping the children busy helped their parents sneak in a dance or two themselves.

Alec stopped the dinner background music and stepped up to the microphone. "All right, everyone. I'd like to invite our newlyweds up for their first dance together. Paul and Kate, let's go!"

Paul rose and took her hand, helping her up and leading her onto the dance floor while Alec played the Natalie Cole version of their song, *The Very Thought of You*. Alec handled the lighting as well, which dimmed around the dance floor while staying well-lit around the children's activities. A spotlight shone on them as Paul spun her around.

All Kate could do was smile and laugh. She felt so perfectly happy and content. Toward the end of the song, he pulled her closer and wrapped his arms around her, swaying to the music.

"Will the mother of the groom and father of the bride please step up?" Alec asked.

Shirley and Justus took their places for the parents' dance, Shirley with her son and Justus with Kate. Alec played a song with an upbeat tempo, which had all of them doing some fun twirls that made them laugh while the crowd clapped.

Since Paul's father had passed away, Kate stayed with her father for the next song while her mother danced with Paul. This song was slower, and she chatted with her father as they danced.

"You two are going to have to come down and visit more," she said. "You have a new official grandson now, and he needs to spend more time with you since he hasn't had a grandpa on Paul's side for so long. I don't know if he remembers him."

Justus nodded. "We will. Your mother and I were even talking about getting a second home here. Maybe we'll spend the summers here so we can spend lots of time with both the young ones before they get too old to want to be around their grumpy ol' grandpa."

Kate laughed. "You're not grumpy."

"I think all us old men are required to say that," he explained.

She laughed, and they swayed to the music some more until Alec spoke up again. "All right, everyone. We'd like to invite everyone onto the dance floor. Let's start with an upbeat song."

The tempo was quick, and several couples stood up to spin around the dance floor. Kate and Paul laughed and danced along with everyone, but after a couple of songs, Kate needed a break.

"I'll get you some fruit punch," Paul offered, leading them back to their seats where Kate sat and relaxed, watching everyone have fun at her wedding. Lexi was still filming everything, running around to different places on the dance floor getting videos of their friends. She also went over to the children's activities, and each one of them happily showed their creations to the camera.

A child began to cry, and Kate turned to see that it was one of Delaney's twins, who seemed to have pushed her toy out of reach. Melody swooped in and righted the situation, putting her thumb up to tell Josh and Delaney that she had everything under control. Kate couldn't help but remember those days, though of course, she just had one baby to care for.

It had been so hard, raising Holly without Vaughn. Kate imagined that her first husband approved of what he was watching from God's kingdom today, happy that his little girl had a loving stepfather and a stepbrother she truly adored. The children had been friends for a long time.

Kate turned back to Alec as he stopped the music and went to the microphone again. "Ladies and gentlemen, it's time for the cake cutting! Newlyweds, please head on over."

Paul took her hand again, helping her up and leading her over to the cake table, which was stunning. Edie had done a fantastic job with the cake, and Macey had added real flowers to the table that blended perfectly into the decorative flowers on the cake.

They both picked up the knife together and smiled at each other before guiding it through the bottom layer, making a small slice that they put on a plate. They set it down and each took a fork, cutting small bites so they could feed each other at the same time. Everyone applauded as they tasted the chocolate fudge, which they'd chosen as their base layer.

"Mm, this is so good," she said.

"Smile for the camera!"

Kate turned as Paul put his arm around her, and they both smiled as Lexi shot a short video then stepped back, letting the professional photographer and his assistant, who was also taking video, move in closer.

Grace stepped in behind them. "Beautiful!" she said. "My staff and I will take over to serve everyone. Which tier would you like?"

"I'll have more of the chocolate," Kate said.

Paul nodded. "Same for me."

Grace cut their slices, and they headed back to their seats as the catering staff served all the guests. Even the children who were at the craft tables were quick to come back to get their share.

Alec put on some soft music while they ate, but everyone was chatting, so it could barely be heard. Kate saw Valerie walk up to him, and he put a loving hand on her belly, which was now getting bigger. Their child was expected in the spring. It made Kate think back to the days of her pregnancy. She wished she could do it one more time and hoped God would see fit to bless them with another child.

Of course, memories of her miscarriage were always in the back of her mind. Hudson, who she'd lost at twenty weeks into the pregnancy, would have been a wonderful older brother for Holly and Cooper. It had been such a devastating loss, just like her husband's death later. With time, she'd learned to accept her emotions and let them happen. It was best to just let herself cry it out when those memories popped up, but she didn't want to ruin the day by suddenly bursting into tears at her own wedding reception.

So, she took a long breath.

Paul leaned in and whispered to her. "Everything okay?"

She nodded, though it wasn't really okay. "Hudson."

That was all she needed to say. He wrapped his arm around her and pulled her close. They'd spoken about her child many times as they discussed their future together as a family. Paul was so understanding, the perfect man to share the rest of her life with.

Though sadness was still present, the happiness she knew with Paul, along with the love of God, was a healing force.

CHAPTER FOURTEEN

"This cake is wonderful," Reid said.

Melody nodded. "Can't get better than Delaney's Delights. Edie has done an incredible job managing the place."

"I second that."

She turned to see Delaney walking up carrying Abby, one of the twins. "Hey," Melody said, helping Delaney with her chair so she could sit with her daughter on her lap. "How are the babies holding up?"

Delaney gestured to a nearby server who brought her a piece of cake. "They're getting tired, but they'll be okay through the end of the wedding portion. I don't want my mom to miss the bouquet toss and all that. After that, we'll take them home and get them to bed, then we'll come back while Mom keeps watch. I think they'll be exhausted after this."

Melody laughed. "Sadie, too. She's been having a great time coloring, but I think she'll be ready for bed about that same time."

"Are you coming back for the New Year's Eve party?" Delaney asked.

Melody nodded. "Yes. Actually, we'll be staying here while my mom takes Sadie home." She looked over at Michael, who was playing on the crafts table with Holly and Cooper. "We talked it over with Kate and Paul and decided the older children could stay up for New Year's Eve since there's no school until Monday. Well, for the other two, they won't have school for a couple of weeks while they go on vacation."

"How are they arranging that with the school?" Delaney took another bite of cake.

"I think they're getting their homework through email," Melody said. "They had a long meeting at the school about it, from what I understand."

Delaney nodded, finishing her bite. "Good. Those two deserve a fun holiday. Even though this is a good thing, it'll still be an adjustment when they all live together. I think Disney World is a perfect transition."

Melody nodded. "Michael agrees and wishes he was going, too."

Delaney giggled, sparking the same response from Melody. "I'll bet he does," Delaney said.

They turned at the sound of Alec's voice over the microphone. "All right, single ladies. This is the moment you've been waiting for! Please line up over where our matron of honor indicates and get ready for the toss!"

Melody watched as a few ladies nervously walked up, all of them giggling and chatting. Isabelle showed them where to stand, and once they were in line, she stepped over to Kate, who stood facing the other way.

Melody had to laugh as she watched Holly march over to the opposite end of the room. At Sophie and Zach's wedding, Kate had caught the bouquet, and she had to explain what that meant to Holly. her daughter's reaction was hilarious. "Boys are gross!" she had said.

Isabelle handed Kate the tossing bouquet, and she did a count-down. "One… two… three!"

Melody watched as it flew into the air and landed in the hands of a young blonde woman who squealed with delight.

"Oh, that's so sweet," Delaney said.

Melody turned to her. "Do you know her? I haven't seen her around."

Delaney nodded. "Yes, that's the new dental assistant who will be replacing Sophie. Her name's Annie. I met her at my last appointment while she was getting familiar with the place. She's very sweet, and she's engaged. They're getting married this summer."

"Well, that's perfect then," Melody said. She looked up and saw Annie walking toward a young man, who kissed her on the cheek. "I love all the weddings we've been having in Charles Town. It just makes everything so much fun."

"I agree," Delaney agreed.

Alec turned the microphone over to Paul. "Thank you again, everyone," the groom began. "This whole night has been such a blessing. We're going to split off from the wedding festivities shortly, but believe me, the party will continue."

Kate took the microphone. "For those of you who need to leave, we are so honored that you shared our wedding celebration with us. You're all wonderful, and we're so blessed that you're here. For others taking children home and coming back, we will see you soon! For those staying, we'll be serving more snacks soon. Paul and I are going to step out in just a moment."

Isabelle leaned in. "And that means we have birdseed to throw! We don't want anyone who has to leave early to miss out on such an important moment. Meet me at the front door if you'd like to participate!"

"I'm going," Melody said, chuckling. "Are you coming?"

Delaney nodded, standing up while Melody held Abby and then took her daughter back. "I think I can throw birdseed one handed."

Melody laughed as they got their coats and went to the front door where Isabelle was forming a line on either side of the walkway. Reid picked up Sadie while Josh held his son, Ethan. Melody handed a little bit of bird seed to her daughter.

"Okay, we're ready!" Isabelle called to Kate and Paul.

Paul took Kate by the hand and led her through the door, laughing as they shielded their faces from the incoming bird seed tosses.

"Oh, that was fun," Melody said as they hurried back in. She didn't want the little ones outside in the cold for long.

"It was," Delaney agreed. She looked at Josh. "We'd better get going. Where's Mom?"

"Right here," her mother, Maggie, said behind her.

Melody nodded. "We'll see you back here soon then," she said.

"Don't eat all the cake!" Josh said as he gathered all the babies' things, and Maggie and Delaney took the twins. His wife just shook her head, and Josh laughed.

Once they walked out the door, Melody looked at Sadie. "She's getting tired, too," she said to Reid. "I'll go find Mom."

She found her mother chatting with another lady nearby, and they said goodbye so she could take Sadie home. "Another beautiful wedding," Sarah noted.

Melody nodded. "Yes, it was.'

"I'll walk you out," Reid suggested, lifting up Sadie.

"Bye, little one." Melody gave her daughter a kiss. "Be good for Grandma!" She watched them all walk out the door and went to talk to Olivia.

* * *

Kate

"Oh, my, that was cold," Kate said, still shaking birdseed off as they hurried into the side entrance.

"Yes," Paul agreed. "I think you needed one of those cape things the ladies wore at Zach's wedding."

Kate nodded. "Those were nice. But we weren't going to be outside much."

Isabelle came in through the inner door. "Oh, boy. It's freezing in here."

Kate chuckled. "I think we let in a bit too much cold air."

"Ready to change?" Isabelle asked.

Kate nodded in response.

"I'll meet you here in a couple of minutes," Paul said, giving her a light kiss before heading toward his designated room to change out of his tux and into his New Year's Eve suit.

Kate followed Isabelle into her changing room where her evening gown was hanging on a hook. Isabelle helped with the zipper and got her wedding dress into its bag while Kate put on her other dress which was ice blue and coincidentally matched the bridesmaid gowns. She'd bought it in DC not long after they'd been engaged. At the time, she'd thought she'd be in a white or ivory dress and hadn't thought of the light blue wedding dress yet.

She looked into the mirror as Isabelle helped zip her up the rest of the way.

"Oh, you look stunning," Isabelle said. "That's perfect for New Year's Eve. And now we match!"

Kate let out a laugh. "We sure do. I really wanted to wear my dress longer, but I'm so afraid I'll spill something on it. I want to save it in case Holly wants to wear it one day. I don't know if she will since it's blue."

Isabelle shrugged. "I bet it could be altered so more white is added. Maybe a layer of lace or something. It's beautiful either way. Not all new brides are wearing white. Or maybe she could wear it to prom."

"That's true," Kate agreed. "It's there for her if she wants it."

"I think she might want to wear this gown, too," Isabelle said. "It's gorgeous."

"Thanks." Kate turned back and forth to see the different angles in the mirror. "I saw it in a window in DC and thought it was beautiful."

"It is, and the color is perfect, too."

Once she was done freshening up her makeup and hair, Kate and Isabelle stepped out and found Paul in the hallway.

"I hope I didn't take too long," Kate told him, smiling.

"I just got back out here myself," he assured her. "You look stunning." He gave her a light kiss.

"Let's get back to the party," she suggested.

The crowd was a lot lighter when they returned to the main ballroom, but everyone seemed to be having a great time. Grace's team had laid out a fresh table of appetizers, and the fruit punch bowl had been refreshed. Their congratulations banner was still up, but there was a new one that read, "Happy New Year," that she knew Reid and Sam had installed.

Even though dinner ended not long ago, and they'd had cake, Kate found herself drawn back to the appetizer table just from the scent. Grace and her team had made simple dishes like pizza bites for the kids as well as finger foods Kate loved like stuffed mushrooms and crab cakes.

"I'm probably eating too much," she joked.

"It's our wedding," Paul said. "You're supposed to have fun. And Grace is a fantastic cook, so we might as well enjoy it."

"I hope she gets a moment to relax," she said.

He nodded. "I've seen her on a couple of breaks, don't worry. She has a big team with her to handle things. Besides, she loves doing this."

"I know," Kate said. "I just want to be sure she can enjoy the ball drop later."

"She will."

"Hey, newlyweds." Olivia and Memphis walked up, holding hands.

Kate turned to them, and they started chatting. After a while, Delaney and Josh came back and joined them. Kate and Paul went around the room talking to everyone while Alec played more music, and they all ate and danced until it was almost midnight.

After a while, Isabelle walked up to her. "The guys are ready to bring it down."

Kate nodded. "This is going to be fun."

Paul, along with some of the other men, untied the rope for the giant, sparkly ball with the new year emblazoned across it that they'd hung the day before up in the rafters, bringing it down a little bit to position it over the base that Sam had brought out of the storage closet. They planned to lower the rope at midnight until it met the base.

"The kids did such a good job," Kate said.

Isabelle nodded. "It's amazing. I'm so proud of them."

Isabelle and Casey had quite a messy party at their house a few weeks ago where Holly, Cooper, and Michael had decorated the giant Styrofoam ball with every sparkly craft item the kindergarten teacher could find. She'd bought giant number stickers to put on it to show the year.

"It looks perfect," Kate said.

Isabelle nodded. "Thanks. I'm glad we did a few practice runs. It was way too lightweight at first. It was Casey's idea to spray paint fishing sinkers to add to it. It's a lot more stable now."

They both turned as Alec spoke on the microphone again. "Okay, everyone," he said. "It's almost midnight! Please gather in a circle around the ball so everyone can see it fall."

Kate and Isabelle both helped everyone get into place, keeping an eye on the clock as the time got close.

"All right," Alec announced a few minutes later. "I'll start the countdown, and everyone please join in. Sam, are you ready?"

"Ready!" Sam called out, ready to lower the ball down.

Alec looked at his watch and nodded. "Ten… nine—"

Everyone else joined in as they all counted down.

Kate smiled as Paul wrapped his arm around her while they counted. "Two… one… Happy New Year!"

Everyone cheered and blew on their party horns, including Holly and Cooper, who were standing beside them. Kate wrapped her arms around her new husband and kissed him. She smiled at him as they pulled back, feeling tears welling up in her eyes.

"It's the beginning of the best years of our lives," he said.

He kissed her again as everyone stopped their cheers and started singing *Auld Lang Syne.*

Kate nodded, trying to sing while holding back tears. She never thought she was going to feel this happy again. And now, she felt so blessed.

CHAPTER FIFTEEN

"Casey and Isabelle are sending Cooper over after breakfast," Paul said, texting a response to his brother next door.

Kate nodded, folding a shirt to add to her suitcase. "Perfect. Mom and Dad are making breakfast for Holly, so both children should be ready at the same time."

"They're both so excited about this," he added.

She chuckled. "So am I. Disney World? What's better than that for a fun vacation?"

"Nowhere I can think of," he agreed. "I'm glad we got the Lion King suite at the Art of Animation hotel. They're going to be so excited."

"It'll be a fun surprise, that's for sure," she said. "Macey said the kids will love Toy Story Land. She and Sam visited that section when they went there on their honeymoon." She looked at her suitcase and frowned. "It's so hard to pack for Florida when it's so cold here. I hope I have enough to wear."

He shrugged. "If you don't, we'll buy something."

"I guess that'll add to the fun." She chuckled. "Mom is packing Holly's bag. How about Cooper?"

"My mom took care of that last week before our wedding," he said. "So he's good to go." He moved closer, giving her a kiss on the cheek. "Don't worry. We'll have enough to wear, and if we don't, we'll get what we need down there. We're just going to relax and have fun. Deal?"

She let out a light chuckle. "Deal."

After Cooper came home, they packed all the suitcases into the car and left to get Holly. She was standing at the door waiting for them when they arrived.

Kate gave both her parents a long hug before leaving. "I hope you decide to get that house here soon," she said, pulling back from her mother. "It's not going to be the same around here without you."

"Don't worry," Felicia said. "Your father has already been checking the real estate ads."

Kate chuckled. "Good. I hope you find something soon. In the meantime, enjoy Charles Town. You're leaving Friday, right?"

Justus nodded. "Yes. We just wanted to enjoy the town a bit more and let the holiday travelers get back to where they were going."

"The crowds should be down in a few days," Paul said. He shook Justus's hand, and Felicia gave him a hug before the grandparents said goodbye to Holly and Cooper.

As her father had predicted, the airport was still busy. "I guess two days after New Year's isn't long enough," she said as they stepped into the busy terminal.

"It's not too bad," Paul said. "But it's busier than I expected."

Despite the crowd, it didn't take long to get onto their flight. Paul and Kate sat across from their children in the first-class section, which gave them all a lot more room to stretch out and relax for the flight.

"I'm glad we went with first-class," Kate said. "It makes the trip feel more special for everyone."

"Agreed."

The plane ride was enjoyable, and the airport in Florida was just as busy when they landed, but it didn't take long to get their baggage. They took an Uber to their hotel, which seemed to take a long time, but the kids loved looking out the windows at all the palm trees.

Soon enough, they arrived at their hotel and were able to go straight to their room. "This is so cool!" Cooper exclaimed the moment they entered the Lion King suite. "There are cool animals everywhere I look!"

"Wow!" Holly ran ahead of him and started looking through the room, but Cooper wasn't far behind. "Look at the neat giraffes on the wall!" she said.

"And the cool table!" Cooper added.

Kate laughed. "Bring in your suitcases, both of you," she said. "Then you can look around all you want."

They ran back and picked up the bags they'd left in the hallway and brought them to the luggage rack, then went back to looking through every room.

"Look at the bathroom!" Holly called out toward Cooper, who was admiring all the decorations in the living room.

He hurried over to her. "Wow! This is all so cool!"

Paul chuckled. "We're glad you like it. We saw the Lion King room online and knew it would be perfect."

"It is!" Holly exclaimed.

"It totally is!" Cooper said. "Are we going to the park now?"

"It's a little late," Paul said. "We have dinner reservations, then we can get unpacked here and relax for the night. First thing tomorrow, we'll head out for some fun."

"Okay," Cooper said.

"We're going to the hotel restaurant," Kate explained. "And I'm pretty sure they have pizza!"

"Yay!" both children said at once.

They headed downstairs to the restaurant, which also got the children excited with its bright colors and Disney themes. The whole family decided to eat pizza, and it was piping hot and delicious. After dinner, they went upstairs to finish getting settled.

After unpacking and getting settled, they all finally got to sleep.

"We're heading into Hollywood Studios in the morning," Paul announced. "So get some sleep."

Kate wasn't sure the kids slept a wink, but she finally dozed off, and the next morning, she helped the kids get dressed and scarf down a quick breakfast before they headed out.

"Where's the car?" Cooper asked, bouncing with excitement.

"We'll be taking the Skyliner straight to it." Paul pointed up at the cars flying through the sky, and everyone cheered.

"Yay!" Holly said, and Cooper was just as excited. They headed to the Skyliner to ride the gondola into the park.

"Wow!" Cooper said as they took in the view from the sky. "This is so cool!"

"It is!" Holly agreed. "Oh, I can't wait to ride the Slinky Dog Dash!"

"I almost forgot about that!" Cooper said. "We need to do that. It's going to be awesome!"

Kate and Paul sat back and chuckled, happy with their children's excitement. Kate looked out the window at the view of the Epcot below as they passed by, so colorful and cheerful. Even early in the morning, there were plenty of families walking around enjoying themselves.

"It sure is a colorful place," Paul said with a chuckle as they stepped out of the gondola.

"That it is." Kate took Paul's hand as they walked toward the gondola exit. They entered the park with their MagicBands and looked around. "Holly and Cooper, it's very busy here, and it'll be easy to get separated. So, let's stay together."

"Okay, Mom," Holly said.

Cooper seemed to think a bit before he added, "Okay, Mom."

Kate's heart warmed at the words. She hadn't realized how happy she'd feel when she finally heard them coming from Cooper. She knew she'd never replace Tonya, his mother, but she knew they could be a loving family together. She thought of something she wanted to ask Paul, but she didn't want to do it in front of the children, so she kept it to herself.

Once they got past the main walkway, they stood in front of the replica of Grauman's Chinese Theater looking at the theme park map on Paul's phone. "Okay, where does everyone want to go first?" he asked.

"Definitely Toy Story Land!" Cooper said. "Our friend Josh at school came here last summer and said it's the best!"

"That's over this way. If you want to see that first, that works for me," Kate said, looking over the map. "There's certainly lots to see and do here. It's a good thing we're here for two weeks."

"Awesome!" Holly said. "I want to go see that first, too!"

Paul let out a light chuckle. "Well, it looks like we have a plan. Let's head to Toy Story Land." He took Kate's hand, and they followed the map.

"Minnie!" Holly called out. She pointed to the character, and they took a little diversion to stand in line to take pictures. Soon after, Cooper was the one to spot a Disney character.

"Sully!"

Paul waved them ahead so they could get in line, and soon enough, they were standing by the tall, blue-fur character for more pictures. Soon after, they reached the Toy Story Land area.

They hadn't been there long when Holly pointed and called out, "There's Woody!"

"Oh, wow! We need a picture with him too!" Cooper said.

He looked at Paul, who waved him forward. "Go ahead," Paul said, taking out his phone for the picture.

The children waited patiently while other children got their pictures taken with the Disney character, then they stepped in while Woody put his arms around them both and posed.

"Thank you!" Cooper said to the character.

"It's his pleasure," a cast member standing near Woody said. "You're his favorite deputies!"

"Thank you," Kate told him before they walked away.

"Look, there's the Slinky Dog Dash!" Holly said, pointing. "Can we ride it now? Please?"

Paul shrugged, looking at Kate. "What do you say? Are you up for a rollercoaster early in the morning?"

Kate laughed. "I'm ready if you are."

"Yay!" Holly said.

"Okay, let's go get in line." Paul put his arm around Kate and walked over to stand in the line that wound around next to the ride.

Kate smiled as they waited. It was fun, seeing so many excited children in one place. While they waited, she watched the Slinky Dog ride meander around her, thinking what a clever idea it was for a rollercoaster.

Finally, it was their turn, and they all stepped into the ride and buckled up. It had been a while since Kate had ridden a roller coaster, but this one didn't look as scary as some of the others she'd been on. It was a lot of fun, holding onto Paul as they whooshed along, the cool wind feeling pretty good in the warm Florida sunshine.

After visiting a few more attractions, it was time for lunch. Kate pointed to a concession area. "There's Woody's Lunchbox. It looks like we can sit outside and eat."

"Sounds great to me," Paul agreed.

"Me too!" Holly and Cooper said at the same time.

They all enjoyed lunch there while they chatted about what they wanted to see next. With so much to do, it was clearly going to take the full two weeks to get it all done.

"We can go to Epcot tomorrow," Paul suggested. "I know we won't see everything here right away, but we can come back in a few days and maybe go through a couple of the other areas."

"Sounds perfect," Kate said with a smile.

"Can we ride the Slinky Dog Dash again?" Holly asked.

Kate laughed. "It was pretty fun. Why not?" The park was surprisingly not that busy, so the lines weren't as long as she thought they might be.

They finished lunch and stood in line again, and Kate enjoyed the ride for a second time. They spent more time with the other attractions in Toy Story Land before deciding to do some shopping.

"Okay, you can each choose a T-shirt," Paul said when they walked into a shop. "And we're going to take one home to Michael too, so you can both choose that."

"Yay!" Holly said. She and Cooper started looking through the T-shirts while their parents waited.

Paul looked at Kate. "Is something wrong?" he asked.

She shook her head. "No, of course not," she said. "This is so much fun. I've just been thinking about something ever since Cooper called me Mom."

"What's that?" he asked.

"I wonder if we should formally adopt each other's children," she said. "I don't even know if that's necessary."

"I think it's a perfect idea," he agreed. "We need to protect their future in case something happens to either of us. Let's get that done when we get home."

She nodded, happy they'd decided to cement their parental relationships.

Cooper ran up with a Toy Story T-shirt. "How about this one for Michael?" he asked.

Paul took it and looked it over. "I think this will be something Reid and Melody will approve of. Is it the right size?"

Kate looked at it and nodded. "Yes, that's what Melody told me. We'll get a toy for Sadie as well. Did you each find something for yourselves?"

Holly held up a pink shirt with Minnie on it, while Cooper showed them a brown one with Pluto. "We like these," he said.

"Okay," Paul said. "Let's get these then look around the park some more."

Holly and Cooper ran ahead a little but still stayed in sight as they explored different areas of the park.

"It's time for dinner," Paul said after a while. "We have reservations at Roundup Rodeo BBQ."

"Yay!" Cooper exclaimed, and Holly repeated the sentiment.

They stepped into the restaurant, where the decorations were so big, it was as if Kate and the others had shrunk down to toy size.

After ordering and getting their food, Paul said grace and smiled at Kate. "We are so blessed," he whispered.

"I completely agree." She smiled and took a bite of her food.

CHAPTER SIXTEEN

Sophie and Zach relaxed on the private deck of their room in the beach resort, watching the sunset for the last time on their honeymoon.

"I'm going to miss the warm weather and these stunning views," she said.

"Me too," he agreed. "But the views are lovely in Charles Town, too, as long as you're there."

"Now, that's super sweet of you to say," she said.

"It's all true." He gave her a light kiss.

"I guess we do need to get back to reality." She stared ahead, taking a sip of her iced tea. "School starts in a week. I need to get ready. It's going to be strange working part time."

"You'll get used to it," he said. "And the program isn't too long. In no time, you'll be working with children full-time."

"I hope so." She leaned against him in the double lounge chair and rested her head on his shoulder.

The rest of their honeymoon flew by in a flash, and before she knew it Sophie was home preparing to see her friends for the first time since the wedding.

"I'm excited to see Lexi," Sophie said, putting on one of her gold cross earrings. "I haven't had a chance to watch all the videos she took of Kate and Paul's wedding, but I'm so happy she did that for us."

"That was nice of her," Zach agreed. "It's also nice of them to invite us to dinner the night we got home from our honeymoon."

"Definitely," Sophie said. "We have a lot of grocery shopping to do. This way, I can do that tomorrow. I doubt I'd find much to cook until we get things organized in our home."

He came up behind her, wrapping his arms around her and giving her a kiss on the cheek. "Our home—I love the sound of that."

"So do I."

He checked his watch. "We'd better get going. It'll take a while to get to Shepherdstown and into the restaurant."

"I love that Italian place," Sophie said. "This is going to be fun."

They listened to uplifting Christian music on the drive over, and before long, they were pulling into the Italian restaurant parking lot. Sophie hurried inside, not used to the cold yet, Zach right behind her.

"There's our favorite newlyweds!" Lexi announced when they walked in, standing before the hostess had a chance to seat them.

Sophie thanked the hostess anyway and hurried over to the table, giving her friend a hug. "You look wonderful!" she said. "Thank you for inviting us."

"And you look tan and gorgeous," Lexi said. "The beach was good to you."

Sophie laughed. "Thanks. And thank you for all the videos. Kate looked incredible."

"She did," Lexi agreed. "It was such a beautiful wedding and a fun party. The ball drop was fantastic."

"I agree," Sophie said. "I loved that part. I have to admit, though, I have a lot more to watch."

Lexi shrugged. "You were busy."

"We were," Sophie agreed. "We had so much fun. What have you been up to?"

Lexi looked at Max and shared a smile. She turned back toward Sophie. "Well, we had a good day on Christmas. I didn't get a chance to tell you yet. I wanted to tell you in person." She took Max's hand. "We're going to have a baby!"

Sophie gasped, holding her hand to her heart. She realized she'd gone too long without speaking and stood, heading to the other side of the table to give Lexi a hug. "Oh, my goodness. That's so wonderful!"

Zach stood and shook Max's hand. "What wonderful news," he said. "Congratulations."

"Yes, congratulations!" Sophie said, almost forgetting to say the word. "A baby—that's so perfect! I'm so happy for you! Wait. You found out on Christmas?"

Lexi nodded. "I worked a shift on Christmas Day at the emergency clinic here," she explained. "I was having a lot of symptoms, and the receptionist thought I might be pregnant. So, I picked up a test on the way home, and it was positive!"

"We confirmed it a few days later at the doctor's office," Max explained.

"How far along are you?" Sophie asked. "When's your due date?"

"I'm only about a month along, so I'm due mid-August," Lexi explained. She turned to Zach. "So, things have changed a little. I'm going to need maternity leave, and I haven't decided past that."

Zach nodded. "Of course," he said. "You have lots of time to decide. We have Annie starting, and I can use the temp service to fill in for you. If you decide to keep working, of course, the job is still yours. If not, we're happy for you, whatever you decide."

"Absolutely," Sophie agreed. "Oh, my goodness. There are some big changes coming for all of us."

"Yes, there are," Lexi agreed.

"So that's you, Valerie, and Olivia now," Sophie said. "Wow. You can all talk about your pregnancies together."

"Yes," Lexi said. "I'm so excited. Oh, and there's one more you don't know about yet."

"What?" Sophie asked. "Who?"

"Erin!" Lexi explained. "She just found out."

"Oh, my goodness. Wow!" Sophie looked at Zach. They hadn't been home long enough to talk to anyone yet, but the idea was so wonderful. Having so many friends becoming mothers made her feel like she wanted to try soon, but she really wanted to finish her early childhood education program first, and she'd just started. "This is all so incredible."

"It is, isn't it?" Lexi said.

The waitress walked up and took their order, and Sophie looked over at her friend. Now that she thought about it, she had noticed something different about her the moment she came into the restaurant. It really was true what they said about women glowing when they were pregnant.

She was so happy for them.

* * *

The front door opened, and Sophie looked up in surprise, setting down her book and sprinting toward the door.

"You're home!" she said, wrapping her arms around Zach. "Oh, my goodness. I was so entranced by my language development reading, I lost track of the time. It's fascinating."

"I bet it is," he said, giving her a kiss.

"I didn't even start dinner," she said. "I'm so sorry."

He let out a chuckle. "That's okay. You're busy! Let's go out for a bite instead."

She looked down at the outfit she was wearing–sweatpants and an old sweater.

He laughed again. "You look gorgeous. I don't think you need to wear a formal gown to Bishop's Diner."

"I guess not," she said, laughing with him.

"Let me change and we'll go," he said.

She nodded and went back to put away her schoolbooks.

"I have to admit, this is a lot to juggle," she said on the ride over.

"Your schoolwork?" he asked.

She nodded. "And part-time work, and being a wife. I think I need to work on my time management more. I should have had an option for dinner tonight besides having someone else cook."

He pulled into the diner's parking lot and turned to her. "Sophie, you're doing a lot right now. Early childhood education is a lot different than working in a dentist's office. So, your mind is learning new concepts. This is just the start of our marriage. It's a time when we both get to decide what we're going to do and work toward those goals together. Remember that I completely support this."

She leaned over and gave him a kiss. "You're wonderful."

"I'm just doing what I vowed to do, which was always love, honor, and support you," he said. "Now, let's go eat."

She giggled as she stepped out of the car and wrapped her arm around him as they went into the diner.

There was a table open close to the door, so they took a seat. The waitress brought over menus, even though they'd been there so many times, they barely needed them.

"Cheeseburger and fries please," Sophie said.

Zach smiled. "I'll have the grilled chicken and rice."

"I guess I am getting into a bit of a routine," Sophie said when the waitress left. "It's only been a month, but I've been keeping up. It's just that I get so wrapped up in the reading assignments. It's all so fascinating."

"And that means it's the right path for you," he said. "You're an exceptional dental assistant. But I've always felt that it wasn't quite right for you."

"That's true." She smiled as the waitress approached with their drinks. "Thank you."

"You're welcome," she said before stepping away.

"But I feel this in my heart now," Sophie continued. "I want to help as many children as I can. I want to spend time with them, get to know them, and give them a place where they can grow and learn, and a place where their parents never need to worry about them."

"I'm very proud of you," he said.

"I'm pretty sure you've found your calling," she continued. "I can't think of anything that would suit you besides being a dentist."

"I've always wanted to follow in my dad's footsteps," he replied. "I remember being in his office and watching the people come in, some of them in so much pain. I thought he had a direct line to God the way he helped them feel better."

She chuckled. "I can see how a child would think that."

He nodded. "Now, I feel that satisfaction not just when I alleviate their pain, but also when I teach them how to prevent pain."

"Our children are going to have the best teeth ever," she said.

"And the best education," he added.

"That's right."

"Sophie? Zach?" They both looked up to see Isabelle and Casey walking in.

"Hey!" Sophie said, scooting her chair over and gesturing for them to sit. They both pulled chairs from another table.

"Hi!" Isabelle said. "Are you sure we're not intruding?"

"Not at all," Zach assured her. "We're just having a quick dinner. I recommend the chicken."

"And I recommend a burger and fries," Sophie joked.

"I'm on board with that," Isabelle said. She and Casey ordered, then Isabelle turned to Sophie. "I want to hear all about your honeymoon, but first, I have news. I was going to call you later. But anyway, the preschool at my school needs part-time help."

Sophie raised her brows. "Really? That would be wonderful."

"It would be perfect for you," Isabelle continued. "I've already told them about you and how you just started your program, and they want to meet you."

"That's great," Zach said.

"Oh, Isabelle, thank you so much," Sophie said. "It's such a blessing to have a friend like you."

"You deserve the opportunity," Isabelle said. "I think you'd be perfect to work with these kids. Anyway, think it over. If you're interested, I'll text you Rose's number. She's the preschool coordinator."

"Please, send it over," Sophie said.

"I have it at home," Isabelle explained. "I'll text you when we get home. Now, tell me all about Fiji!"

They went on to discuss the islands and their resort as they all had a relaxing dinner together.

Later, after they said goodbye to their friends, Zach reached over and took Sophie's hand as he drove them back to their house. "I think you should take it."

"The job?" Sophie asked, turning to him.

He kept his eyes on the road. "Yes. It's what you want to do for a living, so I think this is a great opportunity for you. You'll be immersed in the experience more if you're both studying it and applying what you learn every day."

"I thought about that, but I don't want to leave the dental office without anyone," she said.

"Don't worry about it," he said. "Like I said to Lexi before, we have the temp pool. There's always someone willing to step in while we go through the permanent hiring process. I don't want you to miss this opportunity."

She chuckled. "Well, they haven't given me the job yet."

"But you're as good as in," he said. "I'm sure they trust Isabelle. Everyone knows how good she is with children. If she has recommended you, I'm sure you're a shoe-in."

"Maybe." She laughed again. "But it is something I'd like to seriously consider, if they offer me the job. I'll call Rose tomorrow before my evening class."

"Good," he said. He pulled into their driveway and parked the car, opening her door for her before they went inside.

"Oh," she said, looking at her phone.

"What is it?" he asked.

"Isabelle already texted the number." She texted back to thank her.

"Perfect," he said. "Everything really is coming together nicely, isn't it?"

She turned and smiled at him. "It sure is. God is good."

He wrapped his arms around her, and she smiled wider.

CHAPTER SEVENTEEN

"Okay, Mr. Peterson. You're all set to go." Lexi opened the drawer in the dental exam room. "What color toothbrush would you like?"

"I'll take blue," he said. "The wife uses pink so we can tell the difference."

Lexi chuckled, digging through to find a blue toothbrush and putting it into the goodie bag, as she liked to call them, along with a sample-sized toothpaste and some floss. "Here you go," she said. "Mrs. Wilcox will set up your next appointment at the front desk."

"Thank you," he said, taking the bag and heading up front.

Normally, she would clean up the room and get it sanitized for the next patient, but she was leaving that to Annie, their new dental assistant, who handled everything perfectly. It wasn't surprising since she already had experience in a dental office.

"That's excellent," Lexi said. "Now it's break time."

"Nice, I'm hungry." Annie giggled a bit, which made Lexi laugh.

She'd never met Annie before she started there. Lexi and her husband lived in Shepherdsville and attended the Christian Church there, while Annie lived locally and went to Sophie and Zach's church. But in the past week since they'd been working together, she'd found Annie to be a very nice person with a good sense of humor, so she was glad Zach had hired her.

Lexi led the way into the break room, taking a quick glance at the counter where Sophie had always put her box of snacks. The bags of chips and packaged cookies were gone now since Sophie was working part-time at the elementary school instead of the dental office. She was happy for her friend, but she missed seeing her every day.

She and Annie both took some healthy snacks out of the fridge and sat down. A sparkle shone off Annie's finger.

"I'm so glad he finally asked you," Lexi said. "Any progress on setting a date yet?"

Annie shook her head. "Not yet. We have appointments at a few venues this weekend, so if we find one that we like, I'll know then. I don't want to set a date and then have nowhere to get married."

"That's the best way to do it," Lexi said. "But I hope it's soon. You did catch that bouquet."

Annie laughed. "I keep reminding Hayden about that."

They both chuckled then finished their snacks and cleaned up so they could get ready for the next patients.

"You'll be taking this next patient on your own," Lexi explained. "You'll be in room B again, and I'll take the patient in room A."

"Sounds great," Annie said. "I'm ready!"

They headed up to the front where Lexi pulled files and handed one to Annie. "This little girl needs a cavity filled, so you'll be getting her set up for Dr. Kemper. I'll take Mrs. Gregory."

"Perfect! I love kids." Annie took the file and looked it over before opening the waiting room door and calling in the patient and her mother.

Once they passed, Lexi smiled at the white-haired woman sitting across the room. "Your turn, Mrs. Gregory," she said.

"Hello, Lexi," Mrs. Gregory said as she stood. "I'm so glad you have

Annie working here. She's such a joy. She volunteers for the children's programs every week."

"She is wonderful," Lexi agreed. "We'll be in here today." She gestured toward the first room.

"Okay." Mrs. Gregory settled into the chair while Lexi got out a fresh paper bib. "I do miss Sophie, though. She's always so much fun. But I'm happy she's working with children now."

"She always wanted to do that," Lexi agreed, hooking up the bib. "I'm glad she has that opportunity now."

Her patient smiled. "So do I."

"So, it looks like you're having trouble with that crown." Lexi pulled up Mrs. Gregory's dental records on the computer and looked at her previous X-rays.

Mrs. Gregory nodded. "I am. It's hurting now."

"Well, let's take a look." She brought the overhead light down and looked at her tooth using a dental tool. "Okay, I see the issue. It looks like there's a pinprick hole in the top of it where it wore down unevenly." She looked back at the chart. "You've had this one for quite a while."

"Yes, it's from when Dr. Mitchells was here," Mrs. Gregory said.

"Okay, I'll have Dr. Kemper take a look," Lexi said. "I'm sure we're going to need to replace it. Don't worry. We'll get a temporary one in today, and that should take care of any pain you're having."

"Thank you." Mrs. Gregory smiled.

"I'll be right back." She slipped around the corner where Zach was still talking to the girl's mother about the procedure. He gave her a gesture that meant he'd be in to check on Mrs. Gregory shortly, so Lexi returned to her patient. "He'll be right in."

Mrs. Gregory nodded. "Oh, thank you. It doesn't hurt as bad when I'm not chewing, so I can wait. So, how are things with you and Max? We don't get to see much of the two of you since you're in Shepherdstown."

"It's going perfectly," Lexi said. "Max is still loving his job at the historical society. He's going to be working with the children's programs again this summer, so I'll assist when I can. Those events are always so much fun."

"That's wonderful," Mrs. Gregory said. "I knew you two were the perfect match."

Lexi giggled but then noticed a look on Mrs. Gregory's face that seemed to have a bit of a deeper meaning than what she'd said. "By the way, Max and I thank you for what you did."

"What I did?" The woman managed to look genuinely confused.

Lexi smiled but didn't elaborate, and Mrs. Gregory gave her a knowing look that made her want to chuckle again.

Zach walked in, breaking the exchange, though Lexi knew Mrs. Gregory probably had something to do with getting Max to propose to her. She was more than thankful for her if she had.

The day continued with many more patients, including some emergencies, so she ended up cutting her lunch hour short. She finished with her last patient and sat in the break room for a moment before cleaning up.

Annie walked in. "Are you all right?"

She nodded. "I'm just tired. It seems like the farther along in the pregnancy I am, the more tired I get."

Annie nodded and sat next to her. "I don't know exactly how that feels, but I know a lot about this. My sister had a baby last year. She was so tired all the time, and that happened more often the further along she was."

"I know it's probably normal," Lexi said. "Today I just feel even more drained."

"It's been a busy day," Annie said. "You should probably get home and rest. Or maybe rest here for a bit before the drive home since you need to go to Shepherdstown."

"Everything okay?" Zach stepped in, looking concerned.

"She's overtired," Annie explained. "She should probably just rest before making the drive home."

"Yes, definitely." He sat next to Lexi. "You're welcome to stay here, or come and rest at our house if you need to. Sophie's home."

She nodded. "That would be great."

"I'll take care of all the cleanup," Annie insisted. "Don't worry about a thing."

"Thank you." She stood, taking a deep breath. "I'll just use the restroom and head over to your house."

"I'm right behind you," Zach said. "Let me just finish up in the back room."

He left, and Annie went to start cleaning up the exam rooms while Lexi went to the restroom. She stopped at the mirror, splashing a little water on her face and wiping it off before going in to use the toilet. When she did, her heart thumped wildly.

There was blood.

She rushed out as quickly as she could. "Annie! Zach!"

They both came running. "What is it?" Zach asked.

"There's… there's blood." She put her hand over her mouth as Annie steadied her.

"How much blood?" she asked.

Lexi shook her head. "I don't know. It looked like a lot."

Annie looked at Zach. "We'd better get her to the ER."

Mrs. Wilcox came rushing back. "What's going on?"

"Lexi's bleeding," Annie explained. "We need to get her to the ER."

"We'll take my car," Zach said, getting his car keys out of his pocket. He looked at Annie. "We'll finish cleaning up later. Mrs. Wilcox, can you please lock up?"

The receptionist nodded. "Of course. And I'll call Mr. Renfro."

"Thank you," Lexi said, feeling woozy as she thought about the blood she'd seen. She was terrified for her baby. She'd never been pregnant before and had no idea whether she was having a miscarriage or not, but she said a silent prayer as Zach and Annie helped her out to his car. Annie decided to put her in the back seat so she could sit next to her on the ride over.

"I know it's probably difficult," Annie said as they buckled in. "But try to take deep breaths."

Lexi nodded but didn't know if that was possible. Hearing a buzz in her purse, she knew it was Max. She dug through and found it, pulling out to see his message.

"I'm on my way."

Just those words made tears start falling, and Annie patted her on the back. "It's okay. Is that your husband?"

Lexi nodded through the tears.

"Okay, that means she got a hold of him, and he's on his way," Annie said calmly.

"What if he's too late? What if I've already lost—" She couldn't finish the rest of the sentence.

Annie shook her head. "Don't think like that. I mean, I know it's probably impossible not to. But try to think logically as much as you can. You don't know what's happening. There are some reasons for seeing blood while you're pregnant that aren't so bad. Just keep breathing, slowly and deeply."

She looked at Annie, but it was fairly impossible to breathe slowly as the tears fell. Instead, she inhaled in uneven gulps, feeling her heart pounding faster and clenching her fists as the stress fired down through her nerves. All she could think of was how she needed to protect her child. If the baby was here with her, she could hold him or her in her arms and protect her baby from whatever threat was coming. But at this stage, she couldn't do that. She just kept worrying until she'd worked herself into a panic, her breaths so uneven she couldn't tell if she'd skipped one or not.

"Lexi," Annie said firmly. "Look at me."

Lexi turned her head.

"There are plenty of reasons for blood that aren't a miscarriage," Annie continued. "See? I looked them up." She held up her phone with the search results, though Lexi was too panicked to read them. "What you can do for your baby right now is stay calm, okay? So, look at me, and breathe with me. In and out, deeply." She demonstrated, and something about the way she held Lexi's attention made her focus on her breath. "That's it. Deeply, in and out, and keep doing that. The hospital isn't far away now. You just need to stay calm so your panic doesn't affect the baby. Don't think about anything but breathing in and out."

Lexi kept looking at her, breathing in and out slowly, following

Annie's lead. It wasn't long after that when Zach pulled into the hospital ER entrance and stopped the car at the round driveway outside.

"Can we get some help over here?" Lexi heard him say. "Yes, this woman is pregnant, and she's bleeding."

A nurse helped Lexi out of the car while another rolled over a wheelchair where they sat her down.

"We'll stay here with you," Annie said. "When your husband gets here, we'll send him in. Okay?"

Lexi nodded, still trying to keep up with the deep breathing Annie had shown her. As she was rolled down the hallway alone toward the sounds of beeping machines, she said a silent prayer.

Dear Lord, please let my baby be okay. I already love him or her so much. Please watch over us so my baby can live.

CHAPTER EIGHTEEN

MAX

A ROCK INSTANTLY FORMED IN HIS STOMACH THE MOMENT HE GOT THE call from the dental receptionist. "Thank you for calling," he managed to say before hanging up and dropping the phone on the sofa. He looked around, trying to remember where he'd put his keys and wallet. He'd been glad to go home a little early from work, and since he worked in town and Lexi had a bit of a drive to do, he'd thought about surprising her by making a simple dinner.

But now, all he could do was panic, taking a deep breath before remembering he'd dropped his things in the dish on the dresser, so he ran upstairs, skipping a step with every leap to get to their bedroom faster. There, he grabbed his keys and wallet and ran downstairs, barely taking the time to get a jacket before locking the door and running to the car.

He took another deep breath, fastening his seatbelt before starting it up and backing out, continuing his breathing as he impatiently waited at stoplights and stop signs on his way to the highway that led to Charles Town.

It was the longest drive to the neighboring town he'd ever made. He needed to be there for his wife and child, to protect them in any way he could, and yet, there was a long delay before he could even be at their side. Intellectually, he knew it was only about an eighteen-minute drive. But it was hard to pull any logic out of his mind when it was possible the worst was happening, and he wasn't there with Lexi and the baby.

So, he kept driving, kept breathing, kept forcing himself to pay attention to the traffic around him so everyone could get where they were going safely.

He could only imagine the thoughts that were running through his wife's mind while he tried to get to her. Mrs. Wilcox said she'd seen blood, but she didn't have any more information. He had no idea how much blood or whether or not Lexi was in any kind of pain.

But those thoughts only led to panic, so he brought himself back with deep breathing and prayers. "Dear God, please let my wife and child be okay," he said out loud. "Please watch over them for me and help Lexi and our baby." He knew God was already by her side, and the thought comforted him as he returned to focused breathing and careful attention to the road.

He arrived and parked in the first spot he saw, quickly running toward the ER as he locked the doors. He rushed inside and looked around.

Zach rushed over to him. "They took her back, but we haven't heard anything yet." Max nodded as Zach got a nurse's attention. "This is Mr. Renfro, Lexi's husband."

The nurse nodded. "Mr. Renfro, please follow me."

He followed her, happy she was walking at a fast pace as they passed through a couple of doors. "Is she okay?" he asked. "Is our baby okay?"

"I don't know," the nurse said. "I haven't checked since we took her back. But I can promise you she's getting the best care."

It didn't answer his question the way he wanted, but he knew he was close to being by her side now, which was far preferable to being on the road where he couldn't even ask any questions.

Finally, the nurse drew back the curtain and let him in. Lexi looked up, and her face brightened. "Oh, thank goodness you're here!"

He bent down to her on the bed, wrapped his arms around her, and just held her tightly for a moment. Finally, he pulled back. "Are you okay? The baby—"

"Didn't you get my messages?"

He shook his head, feeling for his phone, which wasn't there. "I guess I didn't grab it," he said.

"I'm so worried," she said. "They took some blood tests and did an ultrasound. The baby is okay for now, but they don't know what the problem is. There might be more tests."

"Okay," he said, sitting beside her on the bed as she scooted over. "Well, the baby is fine, so we can relax and wait for any tests they need."

She nodded. "That's what I keep telling myself."

"How are you feeling?" he asked.

"Okay, I guess." She shrugged. "I'm not as tired now that I'm lying down, but back at work, I was exhausted. It was kind of a long day. Maybe I should—" She stopped talking when the doctor walked through the curtain.

"I'm sorry for interrupting," she said.

Max shook his head. "It's quite all right. Did the tests come up with anything?"

"This is my husband, Max," Lexi explained.

"Good to meet you, Max," the doctor said. "I'm Dr. Selby. And I'm afraid not, not just yet. We've contacted your regular obstetrician, Dr. Williams, and she wants us to do a few more tests, including another ultrasound."

Lexi nodded. "Whatever is needed."

The doctor nodded. "We'll get you into a private room first. The plan is to admit you at least overnight while we figure out what's going on. Once we do, Dr. Williams will decide how to handle it from there."

"Okay, thank you," Max said.

"Hang tight while we get that paperwork going, and someone will come soon to take you to your room." Dr. Selby stepped out as a nurse came in and checked Lexi's vitals.

"I really don't want to stay here," Lexi said after the nurse left. "But I suppose I have no choice."

"I'll stay with you," he said. "I'm sure that's allowed."

"I hope so," she said. "I don't want to be away from you overnight."

"It'll be fine, I'm sure." He leaned down and kissed her cheek.

She nodded, and he rested his hand on her knee as they waited to be moved to a room while she sent Zach a text to give him and Annie an update so they wouldn't wait there needlessly. Then, Lexi handed her phone to Max, an exhausted look on her face.

"Sophie is coming," Max said. "She'll be here in a bit."

"I don't want her to go to too much trouble," Lexi insisted.

Max chuckled lightly and squeezed her hand. "I doubt any of us could keep her away if we tried."

"You're probably right."

Eventually, someone came with a wheelchair, and they all went up to the private room. Lexi used the restroom before she got settled into bed, and she came out of the door crying.

Max's heart pounded with fear. "What's the matter?"

"I'm still bleeding." She laid down on the bed, and Max put the covers over her.

"More than before?" he asked.

"No, it's less, but it's still there." She looked up at him. "Max, am I losing our baby?"

"Sweetheart, no," he said. "The doctor said the baby is okay."

"But what if something worse happens, and—"

He leaned in quickly and wrapped his arms around her. "We're not going to let that happen. The doctors here will take good care of you and our baby."

After a few minutes, the doctor came in with a nurse, who was rolling a large piece of equipment through the door.

"Hi, Lexi," the doctor said. "How are you feeling?"

"I'm still bleeding, so I'm worried," she answered.

"That's understandable, so let's get to the bottom of this." The nurse assisted the doctor, who prepared the ultrasound machine. "Okay, we're going to be more thorough here. I didn't see any problem initially." She looked up at Max.

"I want him to stay," Lexi confirmed.

Dr. Selby nodded. "Of course." She started the procedure and took her time looking in some areas. After a while, she looked up at Lexi and Max. "Did you want to know the baby's sex?" she asked.

Lexi looked at Max. He didn't want to say yes until she really wanted to know, so he wasn't sure what to say. "I want to know," she said finally.

He nodded. "So do I."

The doctor smiled. "Well, your son still looks healthy, from what I can see."

"Oh, my goodness. Our son?" Lexi asked.

Dr. Selby smiled. "That's correct."

Max smiled too as so many emotions ran through him. Knowing he was fathering a son, someone who would need his guidance to become a man of God, made his heart feel like it skipped a beat.

He wrapped his arms around Lexi the best he could since she was still in the middle of the procedure. "A son, that's so wonderful."

Lexi wiped a tear from her cheek and laid back, taking a deep breath, a huge smile on her face. Max smiled, too, but this wasn't how he'd wanted to find out whether they were having a boy or a girl. He'd always pictured a casual office visit where the doctor would finally know for sure and tell them. But now, their son might be in danger, and he felt even more protective knowing more about their child.

Dr. Selby shook her head. "I'm not seeing anything that would indicate why you're bleeding, though I do suspect it's a placental ablation, or a tear in the placenta. But I'm not seeing it here. That doesn't mean it's not that, but we'll need some more time and more tests."

She finished the procedure and stood, giving the nurse some instructions then coming back to talk to Max and Lexi. "Let's observe you for the night," she said. "And we'll take some more blood for more tests. I'll see if Dr. Williams can make a trip here to examine you as well. Don't worry." She patted Lexi on the arm. "We'll take good care of you and that little boy."

When the doctor and nurse stepped out, Max pulled Lexi in for a tight hug. When he finally pulled back, they said a prayer together.

* * *

It had been two days, and the bleeding had subsided. Max had taken time off work for the emergency and had stayed with her, sleeping on a couch next to Lexi's hospital bed.

He stood as she woke up that morning and took her hand. "How are you feeling?" he asked.

"I'm fine," she said. "I slept well, considering."

"Yes, it's hard to sleep in here with all the machines," he said. "Can I get you anything?"

She shook her head. "They'll bring breakfast soon. But you should get something from the cafeteria."

"I will in a while." He turned around and folded up his blanket and tossed it on the pillow on the couch. "I'll just grab some coffee at the nurse's station. Are you sure you're okay?"

She nodded. "Yes."

He went down the hall where a nice nurse the first night he was there had shown him how to work the coffee machine. He put in a pod and made a cup, returning to Lexi, who already had her breakfast in front of her.

"That smells pretty good," he said.

"Do you want some?"

He laughed. "No, I am not taking food away from my wife and son. You enjoy it. I'll go get something later downstairs."

They both looked up when they heard a knock, and Sophie came in along with the doctor. "I think I found one of your visitors," Dr. Selby said.

"Sophie, don't you have class?" Lexi asked.

Sophie shook her head. "Not today."

"Well, I have good news," the doctor said. "Your bleeding has stopped, and the tear is very small. So, we're sending you home. But I want you to get plenty of rest for the duration of your pregnancy. Dr. Williams agrees. You're not officially on bed rest, but we both want you to take it easy."

Lexi looked at Max. "I guess I should take a leave of absence from the dental office."

Max nodded. "I think you should." He'd been meaning to bring that up with her.

"That's a good idea," the doctor said. "Here." She handed her some papers. "We've scheduled an appointment with Dr. Williams for tomorrow, and she'll follow up. The nurse will be in for some papers for you to sign."

"Thank you, Dr. Selby," Max said.

"Well, I'm glad I'm here for good news!" Sophie said. "I'll hang out until you go home."

Max smiled, holding Lexi's hand again. "Well, I guess Sophie can help us with our next task."

"What's that?" Lexi asked.

"We need to come up with a name for this little boy," he said with a smile.

He felt so blessed. His wife and child were fine, and they were finally going home.

CHAPTER NINETEEN

Erin

"Okay, this is incredibly cute," Erin said, running her fingers over a blanket in the store.

"That it is," Luke agreed.

She'd been surprised at how much her husband seemed to enjoy shopping for the baby. Normally, he'd come along for big items like furniture or appliances, but this time, they were mostly looking for things to decorate the room since they'd already purchased the crib and other furnishings.

"But it won't match the décor," she continued.

"And you're thinking of changing it." It was a statement, not a question.

She let out a giggle. "Yes, I am."

"So, we're going with teddy bears?" he asked. "The balloons were nice, too, but I'm okay with this."

"The balloons looked great in that picture I saw online," she said. "But I think teddy bears would give it a softer look. And once we know if it's a girl or boy, we can add pink or blue teddy bears without changing anything else."

"I do like that," he agreed.

"And we weren't having much luck with the balloons anyway," she said. "I mean, this has all been really cute." She gestured toward the items in their cart. "But it doesn't all match the way I'd like it. Is it horrible that I want to start over?"

He let out a chuckle and smiled. "Of course not, love. This is our first baby, so we both want nice things. I just don't want to tinker around too long without getting you time to rest."

She exhaled. "You're thinking of Lexi and Max."

"That I am," he said. "All it took was one busy day at work, and there was a problem. You've been on your feet for a while already today."

"That's true, but it's almost lunchtime, so we'll sit somewhere and relax," she said.

"So, let's put this back and refocus on teddy bears." He started to turn the cart around, and she found herself giggling at the way he'd said it. "Hey, I like a cute teddy bear as the next lad."

That made her laugh harder. "I'm sure you do."

They went back down a couple of aisles, carefully replacing the few items they'd selected that featured balloons. They were still cute, she thought, but now that she'd seen that blanket, she already had a completely different vision of the room in her mind.

Before lunch, they purchased the blanket, a bunch of different decorative wall decals, and several matching accessories and headed to the car.

"All right, so now we want a full sit-down meal," he said, "preferably where you can put your feet up."

"Well, I can't do that in a restaurant," she said.

"Which is why I think we should get take-out then head home so you can relax and eat," he suggested.

She wanted to disagree since she loved shopping, but they already had a lot of things, and she really wanted to see how it all looked together before deciding what else they'd need. "Okay," she agreed. "How about some Chinese food? I can order on my phone."

"That sounds perfect," he said, starting the car after they buckled up.

She got out her phone and clicked on some dishes she knew they both liked. "Anything special you want?"

He shook his head, watching the surrounding area as he backed the car out of the parking spot. "I'd love a few fortune cookies, though."

"I won't forget those," she promised.

The more she thought about it, the better it sounded to have a hot plate of fried rice and sesame chicken in front of her. She hadn't had any real cravings during the pregnancy yet,, but food in general sounded better to her, and the smells were more intense, in a good way. She was almost twenty weeks pregnant now, and she hadn't come across any type of food that she didn't want to eat. That was the opposite of some of her friends who were pregnant, who all had at least one thing they wouldn't go near due to scent or taste.

"I'll get extra so your dad can stop by," she said. "I bet he'd like to help with the baby's room, too."

"Good idea," Luke said. "Thank you for thinking of him."

"Of course. He's your father. I want him to enjoy his grandbaby as much as he can."

The restaurant was close, which meant they got there early and needed to wait for their order, so they sat in a booth and had some drinks. She chose a Sprite so she could avoid the caffeine.

"It smells so good in here." She took a sip through her straw. "It's making me so hungry."

"Same here," he agreed, "for different reasons, I suppose."

She smiled. "I think I'd be hungry in here even if I weren't pregnant."

"Have you heard from Lexi?" he asked. "Is everything still okay?"

She finished off another sip of her soda and nodded. "Yes," she said. "I talked to her yesterday. She's going to stay off work for the rest of her pregnancy, just to be safe. Zach has already brought someone else in, I think."

"Is she going to work once the baby comes?" he asked.

She shrugged. "I don't know. Not when he's tiny, I'm sure, but she might go back later."

"Do you think you will as well?" he asked.

"I'm still not sure." She sighed. "My patients need me, and it's not physically exhausting work. For Lexi, it's being on her feet all day. I'm sitting. But on the other hand, our baby will need me more than my patients. Kate already has some prospects for a temporary therapist to step in for me when I go on maternity leave. That person can probably stay longer while I have some time with the baby. Maybe I'll go back part-time eventually."

"You can take your time to decide." He gave her a reassuring smile.

They both looked up as the waitress brought over their take-out order, so they finished their sodas and left after Luke left the tip. She called his father, Bart, on the ride home, and he was already waiting on the porch when they arrived, having already opened the door with his copy of the key.

"Ah, looks like you hit the motherlode," Bart joked as Luke started taking packages out of the truck. "Let me help you."

"I'll get the food ready." Erin leaned in to accept a peck on the cheek from her father-in-law as she passed, her arms loaded with bags from the Chinese restaurant. She set them down on the dining room table and went to the kitchen to get plates, napkins, and utensils. "Come get it while it's still hot," she called to the men, who came in shortly after finishing unloading.

"My, that smells good," Bart said.

"It does," Erin agreed, dishing out her plate.

"Dad, would you like to say grace?" Luke asked.

"I'd be honored." They all held hands. "Bless us, Lord, and thank you for the gifts of this food and that little one we're all so grateful for. Amen."

"Amen," Erin repeated. She'd become accustomed to Bart's prayers since they ate dinner together often. They were usually short, and, she thought, very sweet.

"Oh, this is good," Bart said enthusiastically. "I might need a bit more of this chicken soon."

Erin let out a chuckle. "Have all you want. We have plenty."

"We got things for the baby's room," Luke explained. "We'll be setting it up after dinner if you'd like to help."

"For my grandbaby? Absolutely." Bart took another bite of his food, repeating how delicious it was.

They finished their dinner, and the men helped her get the plates in the dishwasher and put the little food that was leftover away before they went upstairs. Bart insisted that she not carry any of the shopping bags up, even though they were light. She knew there was no use in arguing, so she focused on getting to the room and deciding how she wanted things to be.

She'd spent a lot of time in that room lately, mostly because she'd been barred from it by Luke and Bart until the paint was completely dry. They'd made the walls a very light green, a nod to their Irish backgrounds, with some darker green trim on the baseboards and crown molding. That was part of the reason Erin liked the teddy bear pattern so much because it had a lot of green in the background design.

"So, where do we start?" Bart asked, setting down the last of the shopping bags.

"I think with the decals," she said. "There's a strip that goes across the top, all the way around."

"I'll do that," Luke said.

"I'll help you keep it straight," his father joked.

"I can probably use that help."

They all laughed as the men got started, and Erin worked on unwrapping some of the other decorations. Not long after, it was all in place, with teddy bear designs all over the room and a few teddy bears in the crib.

"Of course, I'll wash all this, but I wanted to see how it looked put together," Erin explained.

Luke wrapped his arm around her as they looked around the room. "It's perfect," he said.

Bart nodded. "I agree." He was quiet for a moment before adding, "I wish your mother was here for this. Oh, how she would have loved to have a wee one to play with."

Erin inhaled deep, remembering the woman, though she hadn't gotten to spend a lot of time with her. Rose had given Luke both her wedding and engagement rings for her before she died from cancer. She felt honored to have known her and was glad she'd been able to visit as much as she could to spend as much time talking with her about Luke and his life as possible, as well as hers and her husband's. Erin hadn't gone with him to visit his parents in Ireland the time she gave Luke the rings, and it turned out to be the last visit before Rose went to be with the Lord.

"Mum would have loved a grandbaby to hold," Luke agreed, his voice soft.

Erin looked over at him, noticing the sparkle in his eye from the tears welling up in them. It had been so difficult for him and his father, losing Rose. It was even hard on her, though they hadn't had a chance to spend much time together.

"She told me she regretted that she would miss all of this, the wedding, the children." Luke shook his head, and Erin knew he couldn't say any more. She squeezed his hand with the one that now held his mother's rings.

"She's in the Lord's house now," Bart said, and they turned to him. "She's watching over us, and she sees all of this. She isn't missing the child, and she didn't miss the wedding."

Erin nodded. "That's right. Her spirit is always with us."

They stood quietly for a moment until Bart broke the silence. "It's not a sad moment, this one. It's us preparing to welcome this beautiful baby. When do I get to know if I'm having a grandson or granddaughter?"

"Soon, I hope," Erin said. She'd been anxiously awaiting that knowledge herself, but the baby's position hadn't cooperated on the last two ultrasounds. She hoped to have another in the coming weeks.

"Well, either way, I'm a proud grandpop," he said. "I'd better get back. These old bones are getting tired."

"You're not that old," Luke insisted, but they both said goodbye and saw him to the door. He texted that he'd arrived at his house a few minutes later, as Luke had asked him to do every time he walked home alone.

Erin understood why he needed to know his father was okay. "I'm tired too, honestly."

Luke nodded. "Let's go get ready for bed. You and our little one there need your sleep."

She got dressed in her nightgown and brushed her hair and teeth. Luke led their prayers as usual, but this time, he added a few more words about his mother and their baby.

He put a protective hand over her belly as they drifted off to sleep.

CHAPTER TWENTY

MACEY

IT WAS FAIRLY NOISY IN MACEY AND SAM'S HOUSE THAT WARM SPRING day, but it was worth it. Reid and his crew were working long hours to get their newest home addition finished before summer, so even though it was a disruption, it was coming along nicely, and she was excited to see it finished soon.

She was happy to have a Saturday off. It had been almost four months since her busy time around Christmas and New Year's with the two weddings to handle, and in about a month, she'd start gearing up for the June brides.

"I'm glad you came," Macey said to Melody, who was helping her make sandwiches for the crew.

"I don't think I could have stayed away, the way Michael was so excited about playing with the dogs," Melody said with a laugh.

"I'm surprised he's not over at Kate's place." Macey stacked salami onto all the bread slices laid out in front of them.

Melody shook her head, following her with cheese on all the sand-wiches. "They all took a family road trip into DC," she explained. "So, there wasn't much for him to do after finishing his homework, especially since Mom took his sister for a haircut."

"Her hair is getting so long and pretty," Macey said.

Melody nodded. "It is. It needed a bit of a trim, though, to make it easier to handle. She's a very active little girl."

"She's getting so big," Macey said. "I hope we have a little one running around here soon."

"I'm sure you will," Melody said. "And thankfully, it'll be after all this construction is done."

Macey let out a chuckle. "Thankfully. We're adding enough rooms that I think we'll be fine for however many children God has in store for us."

"It's going to be wonderful." They put all the finishing touches on the sandwiches and placed them on a tray on the table, along with some chips and other snacks, as well as soft drinks.

"Lunch is ready if you all are!" Macey announced, yelling over the sound of the compressor for the nail gun.

Memphis, who was working as part of the crew, shut the machine down and called the others in who were out working on the fencing.

"Wow, this is a great spread," Reid said as he walked in. He gave Melody a kiss on the cheek.

"I wasn't hungry, but I am now," Sam agreed as he greeted Macey the same way. He'd been helping with some of the lower skill tasks like holding things steady. He'd insisted that he couldn't sit around and just watch the men work even though he was paying them well.

"We've made plenty," Macey said. "And we have chairs set up on the deck for everyone."

Once all the men put their plates together, Macey and Melody did the same and went out onto the deck with everyone.

"Michael, come get a sandwich," Melody called.

Her son waved and ran over from the back of the yard, careful not to let the dogs out as he closed the fence behind him.

"It's not as much fun with the puppy and Fluffy way back there," Macey said, sitting down. "But there was no other way to keep them from getting in the way of the construction."

Melody sent Michael in to make his plate and sat down beside her. "It's better to be safe. They're both so little and can easily be stepped on or have something dropped on them."

Macey nodded. "I agree."

"We have a milestone day today, Macey," Reid announced. "All the framing will be done."

"That's fantastic!" Macey said. "Great job, everyone. I really appreciate all the long hours you've been working on this."

Memphis shrugged. "It keeps me busy. Olivia gets a lot more writing done." Everyone laughed.

"Is she working on her book again?" Melody asked.

"Yes." Memphis nodded. "But it's a different one. She's writing a book two for one of her favorite stories so the couple can have a baby."

"Oh, that's fantastic," Macey said. "I'm so glad she was able to make that work."

They all chatted while they finished eating, then they carried the dishes into the house. "Would you ladies like a walk-through?" Reid asked.

"Oh, absolutely." Macey looked at Melody. "We'll take care of the dishes after that."

They left the dishes for the time being and followed Reid. Sam walked with Macey, holding her hand as Reid showed them the different rooms.

"It's so much easier to envision it now," Macey said. "It's amazing how many rooms fit in this area. It looked a lot smaller when just the slab was poured, but these rooms are really huge."

Sam nodded. "We'll have plenty of room for everything."

Macey and Melody went back to the kitchen to get the dishwasher loaded while the men got back to work. The noisy compressor started again, but Macey didn't mind at all. Their home was going to be perfect when it was all finished.

The ladies went back outside and walked over to Michael, who was playing catch with the dogs again.

"They're certainly working off a lot of energy," Macey said. "I bet it'll be quiet around here later when they're napping."

"Fuzzy is so cute!" Michael said excitedly, throwing the ball again while the two little dogs ran after it.

"That's a perfect name for her," Melody said. "And Fuzzy sure seems to really get along with Fluffy."

Macey nodded. "They really do love each other," she said. "I'm so glad we went to the shelter that day." She was so glad Sam had suggested rescuing a dog. As soon as the shelter had reopened in the new year, they'd gone to see the dogs that needed a second chance. Sadly, there were several who hadn't been chosen yet, but Macey had felt drawn to the litter of puppies from the stray dog that had been found hiding under a dumpster. The puppies weren't old enough to leave their mother then, so they chose one and came back a few weeks later for her.

"She looks really similar to Fluffy, except she's not quite as fluffy," Melody said. "Did they know what breed she is?"

"Not exactly," Macey explained. "She's definitely a mixed breed, but even the vet didn't know for sure."

"Well, she's cute, and that's all that matters." Melody gave Fuzzy a pat on the head and threw the ball again.

"Mom, can we get a puppy?" Michael asked.

Melody laughed. "I knew that was coming. We'll definitely need to discuss that with your father."

"Then it's not a no?" he asked.

"Not yet, but it's not a yes, either," Melody explained. "A puppy is a big responsibility and a long commitment."

"I can take care of him… or her," Michael insisted.

"We'll discuss this tonight after dinner." Melody smiled at him.

Michael went back to playing with the dogs, and they seemed happy enough, so the ladies went back in to make some fresh lemonade.

"Have you heard anything from Valerie?" Macey asked.

Melody took some ice cubes out of the freezer. "Not since last week," she said. "She's got about a month to go, so I know she's really excited. I can't wait to see the baby."

Macey nodded. "We'll have to have a get-together soon. So many babies are coming! It's exciting."

"It sure is," Melody agreed.

They finished the lemonade and took it out to the deck, letting the men know so they could come take a drink when they needed one. The ladies relaxed on the deck under the umbrella, watching Michael play with the dogs.

"It seems like so long ago when all of us were single and just finding our guys." Macey sighed.

Melody nodded, finishing a sip of lemonade. "I was just thinking that. But it really wasn't that long ago. Now, we're all married, and a bunch of our friends are having babies."

"I hope Sam and I make that list soon." Macey took a deep breath. "We're not in a rush, but all this—" She gestured at the construction. "All this is for the family we hope to have soon."

"I'm sure God has wonderful plans for you two," Melody assured her. "Maybe He's waiting for your construction project to finish, too."

They both giggled and drank some more lemonade.

"Will you and Reid try for more?" Macey asked.

"Mm," Melody said with a nod, finishing her drink. "Absolutely. I imagine we will until we feel we're too old to handle the work of a newborn."

"Same with us," Macey agreed. "It'll be such a blessing to have a family, and a big family will just be amazing."

They chatted for a while longer until Melody eventually took Michael home, and not long after, the men wrapped up work for the day. Once the dangerous tools were shut off, she moved Fluffy and Fuzzy inside.

"What would you like for dinner?" she asked Sam when everyone had left. "I have some of that leftover casserole if that sounds good."

"It absolutely does," he said. "That's one of my favorites."

"I'll make a little garlic bread and a salad with it," she suggested. "Then we can polish that off."

"It's a nice evening," he said. "First, let's spend a little time on the deck."

They took some drinks and went outside where both dogs were napping on the outside bed on the deck, their heads and paws flopped over each other.

He chuckled. "They sure look exhausted."

"Michael kept them playing all afternoon," she said. "I think we caused a family problem over at the Perry household."

Sam chuckled. "Let me guess. Michael wants a puppy."

"Bingo!" She laughed, looking up at the sky, which was streaked with pink and yellow as the sun set over the rolling hills. "God sure does paint wonderful pictures," she mused.

"He does indeed." He opened a soda can and took a sip. "I'm looking forward to church tomorrow. The youth choir is going to join the services. I know this because one of my students is in it."

"Oh, that'll be so sweet," she said. "I can't wait to hear them. Which student?"

"Jayne Sandavol," he said. "And she's so excited and nervous. I told her on Friday at school to just relax and enjoy singing for God. I think it eased her mind."

"That's wonderful," she said. "You're so good with children. I can't wait to have our own."

He wrapped his arm around her. "Me, neither. But I think God is waiting for our construction to finish."

She laughed, happy she hadn't just taken a sip of her drink. "Melody said the same thing!"

"Well, she's right," he said. "It's hard enough just herding the dogs away from danger with all this going on. Plus, it's a bit noisy for a baby to sleep."

"It's a good thing we're getting all this done now, then." She leaned into him, resting her head on his shoulder. They sat quietly for a while, just holding each other and looking at the sky. Their large country property backed up to a natural area, so the view was fantastic from their deck, even in the waning light of the sunset. They stayed that way until most of it had disappeared, and one or two stray stars began to show up.

"Well, I'd better start dinner," she said. "I'm really hungry for that garlic bread."

"Me, too. I'll help."

They both stood, and the dogs quickly woke up at the sound of the sliding glass door.

"Hurry up, you two," she said, ushering the dogs in so she could close the door. Sam followed her to the kitchen where she started buttering some french bread and sprinkling garlic and cheese while he put together a small salad. "You know, even when you were annoying me with fireworks so long ago, I always had a feeling that life with you would be like this," she said.

"Oh?" he asked, stopping what he was doing. "And how is this?"

"It's wonderful," she said.

He smiled and gave her a quick kiss, and they went back to making dinner in complete peace and happiness.

CHAPTER TWENTY-ONE

"I'm going to miss all of you so much!" Valerie gave Cara, her assistant, a hug, or at least as well as she could with her ever-growing pregnancy bump. She had come in to do one client's hair, and it was going to be her last appointment for a long time as she spent time with the baby.

"We will miss you too," Cara said. "But I don't want you to worry about this place. You're going to have so much to do in a very short time."

"I believe it," Valerie said. "I know I won't truly feel it until it happens, but I've seen what Delaney and Josh have done with the twins."

She gave more hugs to the nail technicians and other ladies before looking around one more time. "I hope I didn't forget anything."

"If you did, we'll bring it by," Cara insisted. "You're not leaving the country, girl."

Valerie laughed. "I suppose not. Thank you, and I'll see you all soon!"

She headed to her car, feeling mixed emotions. She'd worked very hard for her cosmetology license and really enjoyed not just the work but the close friendships she made. The salon was more of a community than a workplace, and she was going to miss that. But so many wonderful things awaited her in her future with Alec. She couldn't believe that, soon, she'd be holding their little girl in her arms, cradling her lovingly.

It wasn't that long ago that she'd learned they were having a daughter. She'd been disappointed that the ultrasounds weren't conclusive up until then, but she was also happy that everything seemed to be going well. When they finally got just the right angle on the ultrasound, tears poured down her cheeks. She was going to have a little girl to do hair together and to put into pretty, colorful dresses, and one day, she'd even do her hair for her wedding. They still hadn't finalized a name for their daughter, and time was running out, so she reminded herself that they needed to do that soon.

She drove home with a smile, deciding that on balance, the future was a lot more wonderful than the past. She said a silent prayer of thanks for the miracle of her little girl.

* * *

"Good morning," Alec told her as she woke up the next morning. "How are you feeling?"

"Tired," she said, chuckling. "It's getting harder to find a comfortable way to sleep."

"Well, you're only three weeks away now," he said. "Maybe we can get some advice from the doctor today. There's got to be a way I can arrange the pillows to make you more comfortable."

She shrugged. "Maybe." She got up, and Alec helped her make a quick breakfast before they got ready for her doctor's appointment. It was getting so close now, she'd been thinking about delivery a lot more, with a mix of fear and excitement. She was scared about the pain, and she'd had a lot of conversations with Melody and Delaney about it, and they'd prayed together to help ease her mind. She had a few questions for the doctor now that they couldn't really answer, so she was looking forward to the appointment.

Finally, they were ready to go, and Alec held the car door open for her. It was funny how little things she'd done automatically before, like putting on her seatbelt, seemed to be so difficult now. But she got it on in the right position the doctor had recommended, and Alec started driving them to the doctor's office.

"I don't think we have enough blankets for her," Valerie said. "Maybe we should stop off and get some more. That way, I can have them all clean and ready to go, even if I end up having the baby sooner than expected."

"Okay, but I really don't want you to overdo it," he said. "If you start laundering the new baby things, I have a feeling you're going to do all of it, then you'll stand there folding them for hours. It's probably better to get some rest at this stage."

"Well, I can sit down and fold," she said. "I have to do something. I can't just stand there and wait until I go into labor."

He let out a chuckle. "Of course not. But I've seen your list of things you want to do before the baby comes, and it's pretty long. Maybe shrink that down a bit and give yourself a break. You're not sleeping all night, so you need more time to rest."

She shrugged. "I feel fine."

"Tell you what," he suggested. "Let's talk to the doctor about this and let her decide on a good activity level for you. Would you agree to what she says?"

"I would," she confirmed, then she chuckled. "Would you?"

He laughed, too. "I'll go with what the doctor says, yes. She's the expert. I'm certainly not."

"I'm just getting ready for the baby," she said. "It's a natural thing to want the house just right when the baby comes home."

"It is, but I can do some things," he said. "Let's just see what the doctor says, and then, whatever is too much for you to handle, I'll take up the slack."

"Deal," she said.

They pulled into the doctor's office parking lot shortly after that, and Alec helped her out of the car. He had bought it recently because the truck didn't have a lot of room for the baby, and because he'd wanted something brand new and safe. It was a little low to the ground compared to the truck, so it was a bit of a challenge for her at this stage of pregnancy.

But she got out with his help and sat while Alec checked her in.

"Oh, my, you look just about ready," the woman next to her said.

She nodded. "Yes, I'm at thirty-seven weeks."

"Oh, that's wonderful," the woman said. "I call that the downhill slide." She laughed, cradling her belly, which was about half the size of Valerie's. "I'm Beth, by the way."

"Valerie." She shook her hand.

"Valerie, such a beautiful name," Beth said. "This is my third, and I'm at twenty weeks. You get to be an old pro once you've done it twice already."

"I'm looking forward to that," Valerie said. "You have a beautiful family," she added, smiling at the two small children beside her.

"Thank you," Beth said. "I'm sure your child will be beautiful too. Well, all children are beautiful, aren't they?"

"Yes, they are." Valerie looked up as a nurse called her name, and Alec helped her up. She turned back to the woman. "It was nice meeting you. Blessings for your new baby!"

"Same to you," Beth said.

They followed the nurse to the scale where she took Valerie's weight and temperature as usual, then led them to the exam room, where she took her blood pressure and had her wait for the doctor. "She's going to do an exam today," the nurse explained. "So please change into this paper gown, and she'll be in shortly."

It required a little help from Alec to make that happen, but she was ready when Dr. Williams came into the room.

"How are you feeling?" the doctor asked.

Valerie shrugged. "I feel a lot of pressure between my legs all the time. And my back hurts."

"Is this new since I saw you last?" Dr. Williams asked.

"Yes," she said.

Alec looked at her, his brow furrowed.

"I didn't want to worry you," she explained. "I'm sure it's just normal pregnancy discomfort."

"It might be, but I'd like to check on a few things," the doctor said. "Let's do your exam, and we'll go from there."

She listened to Valerie's heart and lungs then did an exam. "Let's see what's going on with the baby," she said, and she did an ultrasound.

It made Valerie smile, seeing their daughter in there, growing so big. It was only a matter of weeks, or maybe even days, before she finally got to hold her in her arms.

"Okay," the doctor said. "Go ahead and get dressed, and I'll be right back in."

Valerie frowned a little at her tone, wondering if something was wrong. She looked at Alec, who shrugged. "I'm sure everything is fine," he said.

She nodded, hoping he was right. She got dressed, and the doctor came in shortly after that. She pulled up her stool on wheels and sat with some brochures in her hands.

"I'll start by saying the baby is doing wonderfully," Dr. Williams began. "She's well developed and appears perfectly healthy. The problem is your cervix. It's called incompetent cervix, but that's not the greatest term. It means that your cervix is a little weak for supporting the baby at this point in your pregnancy."

Valerie felt her heart thumping as Alec took her hand and squeezed it. "What does that mean for the baby?" he asked.

"It means we need to slow down a bit," she explained. "I don't want you to deliver until at least next week, or later if at all possible. So—" She reached down and held up a brochure. "I'd like to move to bed rest."

"Bed rest?" All the things she'd wanted to do before the baby was born rushed through Valerie's mind. Now, she'd just be lying there until it was time to deliver—and lying there was very uncomfortable.

The doctor nodded. "Yes, I think it's the safest route right now. If you overdo it, your cervix won't be strong enough to hold the baby in until she can finish developing. If she was born today, she'd likely be fine, but we should try to keep her in there a couple of more weeks if possible."

"It's been very uncomfortable for Valerie at night," Alec said.

Dr. Williams nodded. "Understood." She picked up another brochure. "That's why I'm sending you home with this," she said. "This has all the best tips for you to arrange pillows or blankets and get yourself into positions that are comfortable."

"Will I be able to get up at all?" Valerie asked.

"I'm putting you on restricted activity," the doctor explained. "That's not the strictest form of bed rest. You can get up and stretch, go to the restroom, shower, that kind of thing, but only quickly, then you need to get right back into bed. Now, this one—" She picked up a third brochure. "This one explains the activities you can do and how long you can stay up, as well as some exercises to do in bed to keep your muscles active."

Valerie bit her bottom lip, taking the brochures from the doctor.

"I want you to stay on bed rest until you go into labor," Dr. Williams added. "I'll see you again in a week, and at that time, we'll reassess things. I know this is a lot. Do you have any questions or concerns about any of this?"

Valerie had plenty of concerns, but she had to do what was right for the baby, not herself. She supposed that was part of being a mother, but it didn't make it any easier to hear the news. "How will I know if there's... a problem?" she asked.

"If you have bleeding or something that feels like labor pains, call my office right away," she said. "If it's nighttime, the exchange will patch you through to me. I know this sounds scary, but try not to worry. We just want the best possible entrance into life for your little girl, so let's try this."

"Thank you, doctor," Alec said.

They asked a few more questions and finished the appointment, then scheduled one for the next week at the front desk. Alec helped her to the car and got her buckled up, then they headed home.

"I'm scared," she said.

He nodded, keeping his eyes on the road. "It is scary," he agreed. "But I think if we do everything in those brochures, you and the baby will be just fine. When we get home, we'll get you into bed, and I'll sit with you and read all of it."

She nodded. "Okay."

"And we're also going to say a whole lot of prayers tonight," he added.

CHAPTER TWENTY-TWO

"Okay, ladies," Melody said to get everyone's attention. Her living room was a lot more crowded than normal, full of everyone in their group of friends who could make it. She'd told Lexi to relax at home for now, and if there was something she could do that wouldn't overwork her, she'd let her know. "Now, Valerie is on bed rest until she delivers, so let's all chip in and help. I've made a schedule with a little help from Alec about which days she normally does things like grocery shopping and deep cleaning, so we can spread things out."

"That's perfect," Delaney said. "I've already asked Mom and Josh's mom if they can help with the twins when it's my turn to come over. I'm more than happy to cook and clean."

"I'll do grocery shopping," Macey chimed in. "And of course, I'll help with cleaning as well."

"Okay, so let's get some names on the chart and try to spread things out so no one is getting overwhelmed," Melody said. "Olivia and Erin, I think you both need to take it easy as well, so let's have you do some of the easier things, maybe keeping her company and bringing her things she needs. We'll see how Lexi and the baby are doing. She can do something similar if she's up to it."

"I'd love to help with that," Olivia said.

"Me as well!" Erin agreed. "Count me in. Alec has been worried that she's going to get bored not being able to do much."

"Okay, maybe you could switch off days, so this would be the times when Alec isn't there," Melody said, picking up the pen.

"I'll do today," Olivia said. "I'll head over as soon as we're done here."

"I can definitely do tomorrow and every other day," Erin said.

"Okay." Melody wrote that down. "Alec said there are some brochures on the nightstand in their bedroom that explains what she can and can't do, how long she can be up, that kind of thing."

"Perfect," Olivia said. "I was going to ask."

"Okay, so we'll do cleaning in shifts," Melody said. "Some of it will be easy things like tidying up and dusting and sometimes it'll be deeper cleaning like the bathrooms. So, whoever's on for that shift will just look around to see what needs to be done at the time. I've broken that down here if you want to put your name on a shift. Then there's the cooking shifts. I've split those between morning, noon, and night."

Everyone came up and put their names in, so Melody, Delaney, Sophie, Macey, Isabelle, and Kate all had shifts assigned for cooking and cleaning.

"Well, this looks perfect," Melody said. "Thank you, everyone. Let me go make copies on our printer so everyone has the schedule. If something comes up and you need to switch, call whoever is next on the schedule, and we'll go from there." She stepped into the room they'd made into an office for paying bills and made the copies, then returned to the living room.

"I'll call Valerie and see what she wants for lunch and dinner today," Delaney said. She turned to Olivia who would be at Valerie's keeping her company then. "I'll sit with her once I get there and find out what they like to eat so we can start to get a shopping list together. If she's missing something for what I'm making today, I'll just run out and get it."

"Sounds like a plan," Olivia said.

"I'm just happy that her daughter is developing well," Erin said. "We'll get her through this, and soon, we can all take turns holding that little angel."

"Definitely," Macey agreed. "I love how we're all here for each other. It's such a blessing having a wonderful group of friends like this."

"It most definitely is," Delaney agreed. "I'd better get home since Mom is alone with both twins. I'll be over at Valerie's at about eleven. So, Olivia and Melody, I'll see you both there later."

"Take your schedule first," Melanie said, handing her the paper. "I'll see you later."

Delaney left, and the others soon followed after getting their schedules.

"I was so worried when my brother called me," Erin said as she headed toward the door. "I wasn't just worried about Valerie and the baby. Alec seemed overwhelmed. I told him not to worry about it. I said the girls will come through for you both, and that's exactly what's happening. I can't even express how grateful I am."

Melody gave her a hug. "We'd do this for any one of us who needed it. That's what friends are for."

Erin gave her a hug before walking out the door.

* * *

"She keeps this place spotless, as I expected," Melody said to Delaney when she got there to clean. "She's probably panicked about being stuck in bed."

"She is," Delaney agreed. "Olivia finally got her to relax about it. She only wanted a sandwich for lunch, and Alec went to get some work done, so I'll make that for her and come back for dinner later. I've got some shopping I want to do at the boutique here in town."

Melody nodded. "I'll get started on the cleaning. It looks like that'll go fast."

Delaney went back to making the sandwich while Melody looked around to see what needed to be done. Nothing looked dirty, of course, so she decided to do some sanitizing in the bathrooms to start. All the supplies were in the bathroom cabinet, so she slipped on some gloves and got to work.

She thought about her pregnancy and how things had gone for her. Compared to Valerie, she'd had it pretty easy as far as the final weeks went. But getting pregnant had been an issue at first, much like it had been for Delaney. She and Reid had even looked into IVF. As it worked out, God decided to bring Sadie into the world before she went through all the procedures the way Delaney had.

Once the twins came, Delaney had told her all the pain and anxiety from the IVF was completely forgotten for her. It was worth it. Melody supposed that the challenges helped women grow stronger so they could be the best mothers they could be, and as always, God supported and guided them along the way.

It didn't take long before the bathroom was done, so she moved to the other one downstairs before heading up to the master bath.

She stepped into the room to see Olivia and Valerie playing chess. "Hey," she said. "Looks like you two are having fun up here."

"Olivia is beating me, but it's still fun," Valerie said. "And hi! I'm glad you're here. I heard you'd be dealing with my mess today."

Melody laughed. "It's hardly a mess," she said. "I can't even find a spot of dust. I'm just doing the bathrooms, which are also pretty clean, but I figured they'd need sanitizing."

Valerie nodded. "It's been a couple of days since I'd gotten to them. I'm not sure how I'm ever going to repay you for all of this."

Melody shook her head and walked over, sitting on the bed next to her. "You're not repaying anything," she said. "We are doing this because we love you, and we love that baby, and we're going to do anything and everything you need right now to make sure you're both safe and healthy."

"It's what friends do for each other, Valerie," Olivia added. She looked at Melody. "I've been trying to convince her of that all day."

"I know, and you are all such wonderful friends," Valerie said. "I just feel so helpless."

Melody saw tears welling in her eyes. "You're not helpless," she insisted. "This is just a different kind of motherhood sacrifice. I know you have a lot you want to do, so that's what makes it so hard. Right now, we're going to be an extension of you. You tell us what you need, and we'll do it."

"I just had so much planned," she said. "I don't have enough blankets for the baby. We were going to buy some after the doctor visit but—" She paused as Melody handed her a tissue, and she wiped her eyes. "I was going to get some so I could get them laundered and ready for the baby."

"Okay," Olivia said. "How many do you need? You know I love to go shopping. I'll be happy to pick some up, and then I'll wash them."

Valerie giggled through the tears. "I suppose shopping is pretty fun. I wanted to have about a dozen. I know that's extra for one baby. I'll just feel better if I have a whole lot of backups."

"I'd love to get them," Olivia said. "What color?"

"It's the Tiny Hearts Tenderness set," Valerie explained.

"Oh, I know the ones!" Olivia said. "Those are adorable. I saw them when Memphis and I were out shopping, but we didn't have that color in the rest of our décor. I'm so glad someone is using them. Do you have the rest of the set?"

"I do!" Valerie said. "It's all set up across the way in the nursery."

"I will go look at that on my way out," Olivia said. "I've been wondering what all those accessories look like all together."

"Okay, I'll get on with my cleaning duties," Melody said. "This is the last bathroom. Is there anything else you'd like me to take care of while I'm here?"

"Is someone doing the kitchen?" Valerie asked.

Melody nodded. "Delaney's on cooking duty today, so we're having whoever is doing that clean up after as well. Is there something specific you need done?"

"I was going to clean out the microwave before I got stuck here," Valerie said.

"Then I'll work on that as well," Melody said. "That way, Delaney can focus on dinner."

"You are all so wonderful," Valerie said.

"You won't say that when I get my checkmate," Olivia joked.

Valerie laughed, the tears seemingly gone. "I won't mind at all when you win."

Melody left them to continue their game while she cleaned the master bathroom, then she went downstairs and did some vacuuming before cleaning the microwave.

Alec was walking in just as she was ready to leave. "Wow," he said. "You all are amazing."

"We're just helping our friends." Melody shrugged. "And you're one of them. Erin said you were worried, and you don't have to be, not about the cooking or cleaning or any errands Valerie needs. I know you're going to worry about the baby, but as long as she gets rest, I'm sure she'll be just fine."

"I can't tell you how much I appreciate everything you've done," he said. "Erin told me you organized all of this. It's not much, but all I can say is thank you."

"It's my pleasure, and I know all the other ladies will tell you the same thing," she said.

"Erin said you'd say that." He chuckled.

Melody laughed with him. "She's a smart woman."

"It's just that… when she called me and told me all of you were arranging shifts to help like this, I couldn't believe it," he said.

She smiled. "Believe it because we're all here to help."

"I've spent these past few months really getting myself prepared to be a good father," he continued. "Then recently, I found out we were having a girl. So, I started a whole different way of preparing to be the father of a little girl. I'm going to need to show her how important she is and what her contribution will be to the world God made. Before, I had my sister as a guide to what life is like for women. But now, I see a whole new side with all of you and how important all your friendships are to each other. It's been enlightening. I just hope I can be the kind of father my little girl deserves and that she'll grow up to be just like all of you."

"Alec," Melody said, patting him on the arm. "I know you'll be a wonderful father, and I'm sure that little girl will grow up to be an amazing woman." She smiled. "Now, go upstairs and see what that wife of yours needs." She giggled. "Delaney will be here soon to make dinner."

"Thank you," he said again. "For everything."

She left, feeling that surge of happiness for having done her best to help a friend.

CHAPTER TWENTY-THREE

It was a week before her due date, and Valerie had been counting the days. With two weeks of bed rest behind her, and one more possible week to go, it had been taking everything in her to stay positive and keep busy. She'd read more books than she could remember doing before in such a short time. One nice part about that was having the time to reread all Olivia's books, which she really loved.

But sometimes, it was hard to focus, thinking of the things she wanted to do before the baby came. Still, she was thankful for her friends and all their help.

She heard the door downstairs open and frowned, having not expected anyone to have a shift right then. "Hello?"

"It's me."

She smiled at the sound of Alec's voice and heard him running up the steps. He looked around and frowned when he came into the room. "How come no one is here?" he asked.

"It's okay," she insisted. "They're in-between shifts. Isabelle is coming to cook dinner in about an hour. You're home early. Is something wrong?"

He walked over to her and gave her a kiss. "Mom has hereby declared to Dad that I am not to work until after the baby is born," he said with a chuckle.

"Oh, boy," she said. "What did he say?"

"He agreed, actually," he said. "So, I'm officially on bed rest with you." He gave her a wide grin that made her laugh.

"Well, welcome to the club." She reached for her phone. "Your sister was coming to keep me company this afternoon. I'll text her and let her know you're home."

He nodded. "Can I get you anything?"

"I'd like some ice water, actually," she said.

"Coming up." He gave her another quick kiss before going downstairs. He was back in what seemed like seconds, which made her laugh. "You're quick," she said. "Thank you."

"Only the best service for my wife." He wiggled his eyebrows. With the exception of times when he was DJing, everyone thought of Alec as shy and reserved. But when they were alone together, he was outgoing and funny. She supposed that was because he was comfortable with her, as she was with him.

"So, what do you want to do?" she asked.

"Want to watch a movie?" he suggested. "I think I can manage to make popcorn without burning it."

She laughed. "I would love that."

"Okay." He handed her the remote. "You find something you want to watch on the streaming channels. I'm up for anything. I'll go down and make some popcorn in the air popper. Do you want butter?"

"You know I do," she said.

"Deal."

He left the room, and she started flipping channels. She didn't watch much TV other than the prayer hour, but she did enjoy a good, clean movie now and then.

She was surviving through the channels when a sharp pain had her nearly crying out. She held her belly, shocked at first and then breathing through it until it was gone. "Oh, wow," she said. "Alec!"

But he didn't answer. The air popper was already turned on downstairs, and it was loud. Panic rushed through her as she remembered what the doctor had said—because of the cervix problem, she needed to leave for the hospital on the first contraction. She tried to breathe deeply, knowing he wouldn't hear her until the popcorn machine was off. Finally, it got quiet. "Alec!" This time, she screamed.

He was in the bedroom in seconds. "What is it?"

"It's time!" she said.

"Now?"

"Yes, now!" she shouted. "I had a contraction."

"Um, okay." He scanned the room. "Keys." He slapped his pants. "In my pocket."

"My bag," she said.

"Your bag. That's in the closet," he said, reaching in for it. "Okay. Can you walk?"

She nodded. "I think so. The stairs are going to be hard."

"I'll help you down." He dropped her bag. "Just go slowly, like the doctor said."

She got out of bed, happy that she was wearing something halfway presentable, and leaned against him as he helped her down the stairs.

"Ah!" she shouted halfway through.

"What is it? Another one?" he said.

She shook her head. "No, that wasn't a contraction. Something just… hurt." She felt panicked again, fearing her cervix wouldn't support the baby while they got to the hospital.

"It'll be okay," he tried to reassure her, though the look on his face wasn't very reassuring.

Finally, they made it down the stairs, and he led her out to the car. She held her belly, trying to breathe the way she was supposed to.

"Oh, goodness, is it time?" Their neighbor, Mrs. Sherwood, ran over.

"Yes," Valerie said.

Mrs. Sherwood looked at Alec as he got Valerie into the car. "Did you get her bag?" she asked.

"Oh, no! I put it down to help her. It's upstairs."

"I'll grab it," she said.

Alec ran around to the driver's side and took the bag from Mrs. Sherwood as she ran back outside. "Don't worry," she said. "I'll make sure everything is turned off and locked up. Just go!"

Alec was backing out of the driveway seconds after that exchange while Valerie leaned back and focused on breathing. The pain on the stairs was terrifying. It seemed like forever before they pulled into the hospital, though she knew Alec was going as fast as he could while still obeying traffic laws.

He pulled into the circular driveway in front of the ER and jumped out, shouting in through the sliding doors as they opened, "My wife is having a baby!"

Two nurses rushed out, one with a wheelchair, and they helped her into it as they brought her in. "Park over there," one of the nurses told Alec, pointing. "Then meet us inside."

Valerie saw the panic in Alec's eyes as he did what she said.

"Don't worry," the nurse said. "He'll be right back in, and we'll make sure he's with you."

"Thank you," she said.

"You're Valerie McConnell?" the nurse asked.

She nodded, surprised.

"Your neighbor phoned us to let us know you were coming," the nurse explained. "We've got you all set up. I'm Margie, and I'll get you settled into your room. Dr. Williams is also on the way."

"Thank you," she said again as Alec came running up.

"Okay, let's head in," Margie said, wheeling her forward. Alec took Valerie's hand and walked quickly beside her as they got on the elevator and later went through a few hallways to her room. It was pleasant, painted in a soft pastel yellow and decorated to look as much like a bedroom at home as possible. She would deliver and stay in this same room, if all went well.

She prayed that it would.

Alec helped her onto the bed while Margie and another nurse helped her into her gown and got her hooked up to monitors.

"Dr. Williams is about ten minutes away," Margie explained. "So she should be here soon. How far apart are your contractions?"

"Oh, I just had the one." She looked at Alec with panic. "I have a weak cervix, and I… Oh!" another contraction hit her, this one deep and sharp.

"Breathe through it," Margie said, speaking calmly and softly.

Valerie squeezed Alec's hand, and he made a little sound, it was so tight, but he hung on.

"Inhale, exhale," Margie continued. "Okay, good. That's it. So, now I'll time them from here."

Valerie took a few recovery breaths and looked at Alec. "Call your sister," she said. "Ask her to call my dad and sister too. I'm sure she'll tell your parents. Oh, and tell Isabelle."

"Right," he said, nodding. He stepped over to the side a little and made the call to Erin while the nurse asked her more questions.

"She's on it," Alec reported when he stepped back over. Valerie had to giggle at the image in her mind of the telephone tree that was probably happening right now, with all their friends and family spreading the news.

After several minutes, Dr. Williams walked in and did her exam while the nurse updated her. A contraction hit soon after, and Alec was the one to talk softly and help her breathe through it.

"We'll keep checking on you," the doctor said. "When you get dilated far enough, we'll get the epidural in."

Hours passed, and the contractions got closer together, so much so that she felt she was in pain more often than not. She remembered Erin coming in to say hi and praying with her, but she'd left to give the family an update.

The pain was so intense, she screamed loudly when the next contraction hit. "I can't do this!" she said when it passed. "It's too much!"

The doctor came in again and did a quick exam. "You'll be fine. It's time for the epidural," she announced.

A woman came in, introduced herself as the anesthesiologist, and had Valerie curl up as much as she could. She was supposed to hold still, but she feared she wouldn't be able to when the next contraction hit. Thankfully, the anesthesiologist got it in before that happened.

And when it did, it wasn't as powerful as before. In fact, she could barely feel it, and she realized that soon, she couldn't feel her legs either. "Oh, my goodness," she said. She looked at Alec, his eyes drooping. "What time is it?" she asked.

"One o'clock," he said.

"AM? It's that late?" He nodded in response, obviously tired, and she squeezed his hand. "Well, this is wonderful now. Hopefully, the baby comes soon." She finally felt like she could breathe again, pain-free.

"Here's another one," the nurse said.

"A contraction?" Valerie asked.

The nurse nodded. "Yes," she said, looking at the monitor.

"Wow, that's amazing," Valerie said. "I didn't feel it."

The nurses monitored her for a while, and eventually, they called the doctor back in, and she came in wearing gloves, a mask, and a paper gown. "Okay," Dr. Williams said. "When I say go, it's time to push."

"How do I do that when I can't feel?" Valerie asked.

"Just use your muscle memory," the doctor explained. "If you think about pushing, you're doing it."

Valerie nodded and looked at Alec, who seemed quite wide awake now. "You can do this," he said.

She nodded, smiling at her husband. She pushed when the doctor said, and she must have been doing it because Dr. Williams told her to keep at it. It was weird, not feeling anything, but eventually, she saw the wide eyes of her husband at about the same instant that she heard crying.

"Oh, my goodness," she said. "Is she here?"

She'd barely got the words out when the doctor lifted her daughter up over the sheet and placed her on her chest. Even before being cleaned up, their little girl was so beautiful. Valerie put her hands on her and held her as gently as she could. She seemed so tiny and fragile, though she knew she had actually just gone through quite a bit and seemed unscathed.

"Thank you, God," Valerie whispered as she stroked her tiny chin. She could feel the tears roll down her cheeks but didn't reach to wipe them away.

Alec cut the cord. Then, the nurse took the baby so they could clean her up and get her vitals and so the doctor could finish up with Valerie. Eventually, Alec brought her back, all clean and wrapped in her little pink blanket with her cute little soft-knit hat.

"She's the most beautiful thing I've ever seen," he said, "next to you."

"She's absolutely beautiful," she said. She held her daughter close, just looking into those beautiful little eyes that stared back at her. They had to take the baby to the nursery for a bit to get her completely cleaned back, but Valerie took the time to rest. When they brought her daughter back to her, she looked so content sleeping in her arms.

Later, Valerie's sister Kathy came in, then Erin, along with Alec's parents, Caroline and Bruce, joined them.

"Dad will be sorry he missed this," Kathy said. "He'll come as soon as he's feeling better."

Valerie nodded.

"Oh, she's so adorable!" Erin nearly squealed. "I love her!" Alec carefully handed her to Erin, and she cradled her carefully. "So, what's her name?"

Alec looked at Valerie and nodded.

"Her name is Andrea," Valerie said. "Andrea Julia McConnell." She smiled, knowing that her mother, Julie, would have been happy with the name.

Once everyone had a chance to hold her, they handed her back to Valerie, who cradled her in her arms while she said a silent prayer of thanks.

God had truly given them a miracle.

CHAPTER TWENTY-FOUR

It was hard for Sophie to believe that Valerie's daughter was already here. It seemed like just yesterday when her friend had told everyone she was pregnant, and now Sophie and Zach were off to the hospital to see the baby.

But first, they had to make a stop—Charles Town Floral.

"Hey," Macey greeted them as they walked into her shop, the chime on the door ringing behind them.

"Hi! I bet you know why we're here," Sophie said with a smile.

"That I do." Macey reached over to pick up a pink vase. "I can't tell you how many baby arrangements I've made today, and I love it."

"Make a nice big one, please," Zach said.

"You've got it." Macey got started on the arrangement.

"Have you seen little Andrea yet?" Sophie asked.

Macey shook her head. "No, but Sam and I are going by today. I'll probably see you there if you stay for a while."

"That's great," Sophie said. "I heard Valerie is doing really well. She'll probably be home by tomorrow."

Macey nodded. "Erin told me that as well. I hope she's home soon. It was so hard on her with the bed rest in those final weeks." She added a few more flowers, as well as a pink, plastic congratulations sign. "Here. What do you think?"

"It's beautiful," Sophie said.

"Do you want a pink teddy bear for the baby as well?" Macey asked.

"Of course," Zach said. "Thank you so much. This is perfect." He paid Macey, and they chatted a little longer before heading out.

"I'll be there in about a half hour," Macey said. "Just waiting for Betsy to get here and take over. See you there!"

"See you!" Sophie said as they stepped out. Zach held the flowers while she got buckled into the car, then he handed it to her to hold on the drive over. "This is so much fun," she said as he drove. "And we get to see new babies again in a few months for Olivia, Lexi, and Erin."

"I have a feeling you're getting baby fever," he joked.

She grinned, gazing at him. "Maybe. Okay, yes. I'm really excited about starting our family. I know I need to finish my early childhood education program first, but it seems so long to wait."

He shrugged, keeping his hands on the wheel. "Well, you're almost done with your first semester, so it's only three more. That's not terribly long."

"Intellectually, I know that," she said. "But every time I think of holding our little baby in my arms, intellect takes a back seat." They both laughed. She was serious about it, though, and the pink congratulations bouquet in her lap was only making her more excited about the idea.

"I know you want to start a family," he said. "I do, too. We could start trying in your last semester, so that's only about a year away."

"That's not as bad, but it's still a long time," she said. "What if it takes years to get pregnant?"

He shrugged again. "Then, that's what God intends," he said. "He's not going to rush this. We'll start our family when He thinks we're ready."

She nodded. "That's true. So, we'll start trying in about a year, then we'll see what happens. But that doesn't mean I won't stop hoping it'll happen soon."

He let out a chuckle. "I'd expect nothing less."

They reached the hospital and found a parking space not far away. Stepping into the hospital, they saw some familiar faces.

"Erin!" Sophie called.

Erin and Luke turned around, both of them with boxes of food in their hands. "Hey!" Erin said as Sophie and Zach walked up. "Oh, that bear is adorable. We were sent on a snack run. Follow us."

Zach took the food from Erin, and they followed her and Luke into the elevator.

"How's Valerie doing?" Sophie asked.

"She's great, and Andrea's perfect," Erin said.

Sophie smiled. "I'm so glad. I can't wait to see them both."

After a few turns and a long hallway, they made it to the maternity ward and signed in then went to Valerie's room. She was holding the baby with Alec by her side, and Delaney was there, along with a woman Sophie didn't recognize.

"We brought food and friends," Erin announced quietly as Zach and Luke set the food on a table.

"Oh, my goodness," Sophie said in a half-whisper, looking at the baby. Andrea had her eyes closed, and she didn't want to wake her. "What a beautiful little angel."

Valerie looked up. "Hi, Sophie, Zach. I'm so glad you're here."

"How are you feeling?" Sophie asked.

"I'm wonderful," she replied. "I'm tired, but there's no way I can sleep. All I want to do is stare at her little face."

Delaney let out a light chuckle. "I know the feeling well."

Sophie looked at Delaney. "Where are the twins?"

"They're home with Josh," Delaney explained. "They get a little loud for a maternity ward. But I couldn't miss seeing this little girl."

"Hi, Sophie."

Sophie turned to the woman she hadn't recognized before, but her voice sparked a memory. "Kathy?"

Kathy laughed. "Yes, it's me. I know. People don't recognize me with my hair short."

"Oh, wow," Sophie said, stepping over to give Valerie's sister a hug. "I haven't seen you since Valerie's wedding."

"I looked a lot different with my long hair," Kathy said. "But I got tired of tying it up for work."

Sophie nodded. "You're an RN, right?"

"That's right," she said. "I was able to take a couple of days off and left the kids with Doug so I could see my new little niece here. Our dad is sick and couldn't make it, but he can't wait to see his new granddaughter."

"She's adorable," Sophie said.

They both looked back at Valerie because the baby had made some sounds. "She's awake," Valerie said. "Do you want to hold her, Sophie?"

"Absolutely," she said. "If it's okay."

Valerie smiled. "Of course it is."

Sophie stepped forward and carefully took little Andrea into her arms. Her sleepy eyes looked at her, and her heart melted as she stroked her adorable chubby cheek. All her thoughts she'd had in the car about a child of her own came pouring back to her, and she looked up at Zach, who gave her a quick smile and went back to talking to Alec and Luke. She bounced the baby lightly, rocking back and forth as she stood and looked into those angelic eyes.

A year suddenly seemed much too far away.

After a while, Kathy wanted to hold her, so she passed the baby carefully and sat in one of the chairs next to Valerie. "What was it like?" she asked.

Valerie chuckled. "Painful, very painful," she said. "I knew it would be, of course, but at one point, I thought I wouldn't be able to handle it anymore. But the epidural helped. And then I saw her, held her in my arms, and all was forgotten."

"That's what I keep hearing," Sophie said.

"I'm still a little sore, of course, but I don't even care at this point," Valerie continued. "All I want to do is get lost in those beautiful eyes."

"It happens every time," Kathy said, handing Andrea back to Valerie. "You think that once you've had one, that you'll get used to that and won't be so mesmerized by them, but nope, it happens again."

"I'm sure it does," Sophie said.

They chatted for several minutes before a nurse popped her head into the room. "You're getting a crowd of visitors out there," she said with a smile. "We need to keep the number down in here, so maybe everyone could take turns. The others are in the waiting room."

"Zach and I will head out," Sophie said, stroking Andrea's cheek again. "She's so beautiful. Congratulations."

"Thank you," Valerie said, her smile wide.

Zach added his congratulations, and they went out to the waiting room, where several of their friends were gathered.

"Hey," Macey said. "Is it our turn?"

"Go ahead," Sophie said. "She's the most beautiful little girl ever."

"I'm sure of it!" Macey and Sam went back to Valerie's room while Sophie sat by Melody.

"How's she doing?" Melody asked.

"She looks great." Sophie looked up as Erin and Luke came out.

"We don't want to keep anyone from getting a turn," Erin said. "Who's next?"

Melody looked at Olivia and Isabelle. "Go ahead, Melody," Olivia said.

"Then I guess it's my turn," she said.

Zach started chatting with Luke again, and Olivia sat beside Sophie. "Did it give you any ideas?" she said with a grin.

"Of course it did," Sophie said. "But I have to wait until I'm almost done with school to try."

Olivia nodded. "That's a good plan. That way, you'll have that done for when you're ready to start working later, after the baby."

They both looked up as Macey, Sam, Melody, and Delaney walked out from Valerie's room. "The baby needs to eat," Delaney explained. "And I need to get back to my own little ones. Have fun, everyone!"

"Bye, Delaney," Sophie said as her friend walked out. She turned to the others. "Olivia and Erin, how have you two been feeling?" The men had moved over to the side, so she felt comfortable asking.

"I'm not sick often anymore," Erin said. "But I'm getting weird cravings. I need ice cream almost constantly." She giggled.

"There's nothing weird about ice cream," Sophie said with a laugh.

"No, not until you crave mixed flavors," she explained. "I send Luke to the store for the oddest combinations."

"You sound like me," Kathy said with a laugh.

"I think we all like ice cream," Melody said. "But I wanted a lot of it when I was pregnant, too… that and pancakes."

"Mm, that sounds amazing," Erin said.

"I just want to eat everything," Olivia said. "But I try to keep it reasonable. I'm eating for two, not twelve." They all let out a chuckle.

"You know, it's been so much fun doing things together now that we're all married," Macey said. "Our conversations have turned from wondering whether our men would pop the question to talking about the best ice cream flavors for pregnancy."

"That's very true," Sophie said. "I guess that's how life changes over time. I feel so different now that I'm Mrs. Kemper, though I'll always be the same person. I don't know if that makes sense."

"Of course it does," Melody said. "Our priorities change when we're married. And when it happens to all our friends, those friendships change too—for the better."

"I love how we all pulled together to help Valerie," Erin said. "That was the power of friendship and God's love in action."

"Definitely," Sophie agreed.

They chatted for a while longer, with each taking more turns seeing the baby quickly before they all decided that Valerie needed her rest.

Zach held the car door open for Sophie when it was their turn to leave. "I saw that look in your eyes when you held that baby," he said.

She chuckled. "I was hoping you had. It's always such an amazing experience seeing new life. I couldn't help hoping we have our first child as soon as we can."

"I hope for the same thing," he agreed. He closed the door and went around to the driver's side. "I still think you should have most of your schooling finished before we try. That way, it'll be done, something you can go back to if you decide that's right for you after the baby."

"Then again, I might just decide that we need a bigger family, so I wouldn't go back to work," she said. "If that's the case, I'd want to try again as soon as I'm able. I really enjoy my part-time work with the children now, but I'm not certain I'd want to go back to work after having our own."

He nodded as he backed the car out and headed down the road toward their house. "If you decide never to work outside the home again, you know I fully support you. And if you want to work with children when you're ready, I'll support that, too. But I do think that in the meantime, having that education will help with our own children, so it still has value even if you decide never to pursue it as a career."

"Thank you," she said. "You're the best husband ever."

She was so thankful to God for everything she had in life, especially Zach.

CHAPTER TWENTY-FIVE

"CAN I HAVE SOME MORE EGGS, PLEASE?" MICHAEL ASKED.

Melody passed her son the plate of scrambled eggs. "Yes, but finish them quickly. We have to leave to get you to baseball practice in a half an hour."

"Yes, Mom."

"Do you have a game this weekend?" Reid asked, taking another bite of his own breakfast.

"Yes, against the Panthers," Michael explained. "Are you coming, Dad?"

Reid nodded, finishing his bite. "Of course. We'll all be there to cheer on our favorite first baseman."

"Awesome!" Michael took some more eggs, passed the plate back, and scarfed down a few more bites.

Melody helped Sadie, who was sitting beside her in her booster seat, get some more eggs as well. They all chatted as they ate.

"Are you excited about starting school again?" Melody asked

Michael. It was almost the end of July now, so classes would be starting in about a month.

"Yes!" Michael said. "I get to be in Mr. Abernathy's math class now, and that's so cool!"

Reid chuckled as he nodded. "It sure is. He's a great teacher."

After a while, Reid finished his last bite. "I'd better get going. We're getting the concrete poured on Henry Wilson's new garage addition today."

"That's great," Melody said. "I know he was so excited to get a new workshop. Linda and I were chatting in church, and she said he's been waiting to start this for quite a while. He wants to set up all his wood-working equipment in one place."

"It's a big expansion." Reid stood and gave her a kiss on the cheek. "I'll see you at dinner. Michael and Sadie, be good for your mother and have a fun day."

"Bye, honey," Melody said.

Michael hurriedly finished a bite. "Bye, Dad!"

"Bye, Daddy," Sadie said, waving.

Reid gave each of the children a quick kiss on the tops of their heads and headed out.

"Okay, Michael, are you finished?" Melody asked.

"One more bite." He scooped a big bite into his mouth.

Melody chuckled. "Go get ready, and I'll clean up and get Sadie ready." She looked at her daughter. "We're going shopping!"

"Shop!" Sadie repeated, waving her arms excitedly.

Melody smiled, making quick work of gathering all the plates and getting them into the dishwasher while Sadie finished a few more bites. Once done, she helped her down and added her plate, turning on the dishwasher and heading upstairs with her daughter to get her ready for the day.

"I'm ready, Mom!" Michael called from his room.

"Okay," she said. "Come keep an eye on your sister while I freshen up and get my purse."

Not long after, they were out the door, on their way to the school's baseball field. Melody waved at Kate, who was setting out snacks. It would be Melody's turn to supply them for the game on Saturday. Cooper came running up to meet Michael, who grabbed his gear and went over to talk with him excitedly before walking over to their coach.

Kate walked up. "Hey, how's your day going?" she asked.

"Perfectly." Melody nodded toward Sadie, who was still buckled in. "We're heading out for some grocery shopping, then we'll come watch Michael practice for a bit."

"Oh, can you do me a favor and pick up some cinnamon?" Kate asked. "I'm making some rolls tonight and that's the only thing I need. It'll save me a trip." She reached into her purse and handed Melody some money.

"Of course," Melody said. "I'll bring it right back."

The two women chatted for a few minutes, then Melody headed to the store. It was starting to be a bit more challenging since Sadie walked beside her now instead of riding in the cart, but her three-year-old was getting used to staying beside her and not grabbing things off the shelves. Melody picked out a roast for dinner, turning around to see a woman walk by with a young baby.

"Oh, how adorable," she said, looking at the sweet face peeking out from the pink blanket. "How old is she?"

"Three months," the mother said. "Your little girl is adorable, too."

"Thank you," Melody said. "Be sure to enjoy this time. They grow up so quickly." She couldn't help thinking that maybe, right at this moment, she was pregnant again. She'd spent all day trying not to think about her doctor's appointment the next day, trying not to get too excited about the possibility.

"I will," the woman said.

She finished her shopping and went home to get it all put away while Sadie played with her toys, then they headed back out to the ball field, just in time to see Michael make a hit that went far out into center field.

"Great job!" Melody called from the stands.

After a while, practice was over and they all headed home where Melody started dinner. As she chopped vegetables for the side dish, she thought about how busy things were now that she was a mother of two, wondering if it would be possible to fit even more into every day. She decided that since a lot of women did it, she could, too.

Reid came home right as dinner was ready, and he said grace before they had a nice family dinner together. Later that night, she couldn't hold in her excitement anymore.

"I hope it's positive," she said. "I'm so excited about this doctor's appointment."

He chuckled as he put his shoes in the closet. "I know, so am I. You've probably been excited all day, haven't you?"

"I have," she said. "But I had so much to do, I had to concentrate on that. Now, I have time to think about it. I can't help wondering if it'll be a boy or a girl."

He laughed again, giving her a quick kiss. "Let's find out for sure that you're pregnant before getting too excited about decorating the nursery again."

"I'll try, but no promises." She giggled. "I'm glad we have a big house or else your crew would be working on a big project right now."

"We have plenty of rooms," he said. "And I'm happy about that, too. Let's include our possible new baby in our prayers tonight."

"I'd love that," she said.

His words were beautiful that night as he asked God to bless their new child, if it was His will to send them one.

* * *

MELODY'S MOTHER SEEMED JUST AS EXCITED AS SHE WAS WHEN THEY dropped off Michael and Sadie that morning.

"I said a prayer for you last night," Sarah whispered as the kids ran in to play with the toys their grandmother kept at her house.

"Thank you," Melody said. "We did as well. It's still up to God's will, but I can't help being excited."

"Well, I hope you have some good news to tell the children when you get back," Sarah said.

"I hope so, too." They got in the car and headed to the medical center.

The fear of uncertainty mixed with excitement rushed through her as she and Reid sat in the waiting room at Dr. Paulson's office. She was so nervous, Reid had offered to fill out the updated paperwork. She'd already been following all the instructions Dr. Paulson had given her when she was pregnant with Sadie, just in case. She wanted to be sure their next child had the best start possible from the very beginning.

She glanced over at a woman sitting next to her and noticed her hands were shaking. "I hope all is well," Melody told her.

She looked up. "Oh, yes, it is. Thank you. I'm just so nervous because I'm going to find out today whether I'm pregnant, and my husband couldn't get time away from his job."

Melody nodded, imagining the difficulty the woman was facing without her husband present to support her. "I'm sure he's praying for you," she said.

The woman nodded. "I know he is. I'm just so excited and worried at the same time. My name is Lisa, by the way. Are you expecting?"

"I'm Melody," she said. "And we're going to find out the same thing today."

"Oh, that's wonderful," Lisa said. "I hope it's a yes. You seem like such nice people. Would this be your first?"

"We already have a boy and a girl," Melody explained.

"That's fantastic," Lisa said. "I hope mine is a yes, and that this is just the first of many. We want a big family."

"Then we'll be praying for you to have that," Melody said.

Lisa smiled. "Thank you so much."

A nurse opened the waiting room door and called Lisa back. "Good luck!" Melody said.

"You, too." Lisa looked calmer as she stepped through the door.

Reid squeezed her hand. "It'll be our turn next," he said.

She nodded, feeling a bit calmer after talking to Lisa, whose husband couldn't be with her. She had Reid right beside her.

Eventually, the nurse called her name, and they went back into the exam room area, where the nurse took her weight and temperature. She escorted them to an exam room toward the back.

"I'm Pamela," she said when she closed the door behind them. "I'm fairly new here, so I haven't had the pleasure of meeting you yet."

"I'm Melody," she said, but then she giggled. "I suppose you know that. This is my husband, Reid."

"It's good to meet you both." Pamela smiled as she turned on the computer and started entering information. "Okay, let's get your blood pressure."

Melody tried to relax as the arm cuff squeezed tighter, but she was so excited about the possibilities, it wasn't easy. In the end, the result was slightly higher than normal.

"That's usually fine," Pamela said. "But I'll let the doctor know. I'm sure you're just excited about your answer today."

"Yes," Melody said, chuckling.

Pamela finished adding information. "Dr. Paulson will be right in, but first, let's get your sample."

She took a deep breath and followed Pamela to the restroom where she went through the motions to collect her sample and put it in the special cabinet in the wall. She quickly headed back to Reid.

He put his arms around her the moment she stepped back into the exam room. "We'll know soon," he said.

She nodded, taking a deep breath again. "Oh, I hope it's a yes."

"Me, too," he agreed.

In a few minutes, the doctor knocked on the door.

"Melody, Reid, it's so good to see you again," Dr. Paulson said. "I understand you're hoping for child number three."

"We sure are," Melody said.

She thought back to how she'd felt for the many months they'd been trying to get pregnant with Sadie. She loved Michael with all her heart, but it had been time for them to try to expand their family. She'd been so excited then, too, but that excitement ended in disappointment every month. After their one-year wedding anniversary, she still wasn't pregnant. They'd discussed IVF with the doctor, but when Reid's business got busier, they'd put it on the sidelines.

Eventually, the results had come back positive, and they had their precious Sadie. Now, she prayed it would happen for them again, if it was God's will.

The doctor looked at her and smiled. "Congratulations. You're pregnant."

Melody hitched a breath at the words. "I'm pregnant?"

"Yes, you are," the doctor confirmed.

Melody looked at Reid, instantly feeling the tears well up in her eyes. "We're pregnant again!"

"Yes, we are!" He pulled her into a hug. "This is the best news I've heard since… well, since the last time I heard it." They all laughed, including Dr. Paulson.

"Now, remember that we still have the same obstacles that were part of your first pregnancy," the doctor said. "But having delivered before, I think we can be much more optimistic this time."

"Thank you," Melody said. "Thank you so much!"

The tears of happiness fell before she could stop them. It was the beginning of a new chapter in their lives, with an even bigger family. Her days would be busier, but they would be filled with love and gratitude.

The first time she found out she was pregnant, she'd wanted to hold back the information, worried something would happen. But now, she wanted to tell everyone. Her circle of friends had grown in Charles Town, and their friendships were strong. They'd all been brides now, and several of them were on the path of starting families. Olivia, Erin, and Lexi were all expecting their children to be born very soon. Now, she was growing her own family.

She looked at Reid. "Everything is so wonderful," she said. "God is so wonderful."

"That He is," he agreed. "I love you, Melody."

"I love you, Reid," she said. "Let's get started on this new adventure together."

THE END.

A NOTE FROM THE AUTHOR

Hi everyone!

I just wanted to thank you for reading The Charles Town Bride series. I hope that you've enjoyed these books!

Since I first wrote *Melody's Christmas* in 2017, I've had these gals in my life. It's strange to think it might all be over now.

But it doesn't have to be. If you've enjoyed the series, please leave a review and share with your friends. If there's enough demand, I'll happily write another series about the women of Charles Town raising their kids—Charles Town Moms.

Let me know your thoughts in the reviews, and thanks again!

Love,

Immy

ALSO BY ID JOHNSON

Stand Alone Titles

<u>All I Want for Christmas is Pooch</u>

(*<u>sweet contemporary romance</u>*)

<u>Christmas Memory</u>

(*<u>sweet contemporary romance</u>*)

<u>The Doll Maker's Daughter at Christmas</u>

(*clean romance/historical*)

<u>Pretty Little Monster</u>

(*young adult/suspense*)

<u>The Journey to Normal: Our Family's Life with Autism</u> (*nonfiction*)

<u>Found by the Alpha (fantasy romance)</u>

Love Throughout Time

(*time travel romance*)

Back to Titanic

Back to Gettysburg

Back to Bunker Hill

Back to the Highlands

Back to Port Royal (coming soon!)

Silverwood Academy

(*paranormal romance*)

Vampire Hunter

World Builder

Realm Jumper

Celestial Springs

(psychological thriller/literary fiction/women's fiction)

<u>Beneath the Inconstant Moon</u>

<u>The First Mrs. Edwards</u>

<u>Leaving Ginny</u>

The Motherhood

(dystopian romance)

<u>Rain's Rebellion</u>

<u>Rain's Run</u>

<u>Rain's Return</u>

Ashes and Rose Petals

(contemporary romance/retelling of Romeo and Juliet and Cinderella)

<u>Girl in the Attic</u>

<u>Girl From the Tomb</u>

<u>Girl On the Beach</u>

Nashville Country Dreams

(contemporary romance)

<u>Meant to Marry Me</u>

<u>Lead Me Home</u>

<u>You Are the Reason</u>

Forever Love series

(clean romance/historical)

<u>Cordia's Will: A Civil War Story of Love and Loss</u>

<u>Cordia's Hope: A Story of Love on the Frontier</u>

The Clandestine Saga series

(paranormal romance)

Transformation

Resurrection

Repercussion

Absolution

Illumination

Destruction

Annihilation

Obliteration

Termination

A Vampire Hunter's Tale (based on The Clandestine Saga)

(paranormal/alternate history)

Aaron

Jamie

Elliott

Christian

The Chronicles of Cassidy (based on The Clandestine Saga)

(young adult paranormal)

So You Think Your Sister's a Vampire Hunter?

Who Wants to Be a Vampire Hunter?

How Not to Be a Vampire Hunter

My Life As a Teenage Vampire Hunter

Vampire Hunting Isn't for Morons

Vampires Bite and Other Life Lessons

Gone Guardian

Death Does Not Become Her

Blood of the Vampire Hunter (based on The Clandestine Saga)

(paranormal romance)

Night Slayer

Shadow Stalker

Queen Catcher

Mother Hunter

Father Finder

Ghosts of Southampton series

(historical romance)

Prelude

Titanic

Residuum

Lusitania

Heartwarming Holidays Sweet Romance series

(Christian/clean romance)

Melody's Christmas

Christmas Cocoa

Winter Woods

Waiting On Love

Shamrock Hearts

A Blossoming Spring Romance

Firecracker!

Falling in Love

Thankful for You

Melody's Christmas Wedding

The New Year's Date

Charles Town Brides (based on Heartwarming Holidays Sweet Romance)

(Christian/clean romance)

From This Moment

Can't Help Falling in Love

<u>It's Your Love</u>

<u>When You Say Nothing At All</u>

<u>My Girl</u>

<u>Unchained Melody</u>

<u>I Only Have Eyes For You</u>

<u>At Last</u>

<u>The Very Thought of You</u>

Reaper's Hollow

(paranormal/urban fantasy)

<u>Ruin's Lot</u>

<u>Ruin's Promise</u>

<u>Ruin's Legacy</u>

When Kings Collide

(steamy historical romance)

<u>Princess of Silence</u>

<u>Princess of Hearts</u>

Collections

<u>Ghosts of Southampton Books 0-2</u>

<u>Reaper's Hollow Books 1-3</u>

<u>The Clandestine Saga Books 1-3</u>

<u>The Chronicles of Cassidy Books 1-4</u>

<u>Celestial Springs Collection</u>

<u>Heartwarming Holidays Sweet Romance Books 1-3</u>

<u>Heartwarming Holidays Sweet Romance Books 4-7</u>

Websites: https://books2read.com/ap/xX7ZD8/ID-Johnson

For updates, visit www.authoridjohnson.blogspot.com

Follow on Twitter @authoridjohnson

Find me on Facebook at www.facebook.com/IDJohnsonAuthor

Instagram: @authoridjohnson

Follow me on Bookbub: https://www.bookbub.com/authors/id-johnson

www.ingramcontent.com/pod-product-compliance
Lightning Source LLC
Chambersburg PA
CBHW060316310726

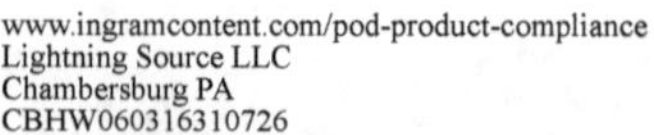

48976CB00007B/2344